I0533988

Deranged Justice

A Sheriff Lexie Wolfe Novel

Book 5, 2nd Edition

DONNA WELCH JONES

Twisted Plot Publishing

Deranged Justice is a work of fiction. Names, characters, places, and incidents are products of the author's imagination or are used fictitiously and are not to be construed as real. Any resemblance to actual events, locales, organizations, or persons, living or dead, is entirely coincidental.

Twisted Plot Publishing
© 2017, Donna Welch Jones
21938 So. Hickory Lane
Tahlequah, Oklahoma 74464
Printed in the United States of America

ISBN: 978-0-9970148-3-9: Paperback

Visit the authors' website: www.donnawelchjones.com

DEDICATION

To My Favorite Guys
Marcus Jones, Eddie Welch, Steven Roberts,
Joseph Welch, Micah Jones, Brian Price,
Todd Chapman, Michael Kurle, Matt Jones

CHAPTER ONE

Mayor Clayton's words pierced across Dixie's restaurant as Sheriff Lexie walked in the door.

"Come in Sheriff," Clayton's mouth tightened to an ugly smirk. "Even people on death row get a last meal. Let me pay for your dinner since you'll lose your job tonight."

Laughter from restaurant customers rippled to her ears.

Lexie glanced at the table where Clayton sat with her opposition, Barney Sims, better known as Slick. The two men were an unlikely pair of friends. Their similarity ended with heights around six feet. Clayton's clean-shaven face contrasted with Slick's stiff handlebar mustache. Slick's boots were marked by dirt spots and worn patches. Clayton's shoes were so shiny they reflected the overhead light. Clayton's salt and pepper hair was side swept and sprayed to perfection. Slick's oily hair was parted down the middle and emphasized his doughy nose. The men's scornful expressions didn't fit in the red and white gingham décor of Dixie's cheery eatery.

Lexie turned to the cash register and met Gina's pleased expression. *My ex fiancé's new wife is enjoying my humiliation.* "Is my to go order ready?"

The sting of Gina's words carried across the room. "You might as well sit and eat your last meal as sheriff with your friends."

Clayton and Slick's laughter reached Lexie's ears. She slowly exhaled in an attempt to keep her anger from seeping out.

"Come on, ex-sheriff," Clayton chirped, "join us and give Slick an update on sheriff business to make his transition easier on January 1."

Lexie caught sight of the owner through the serving window. "Dixie," she called, "is my takeout ready?"

Dixie's steps ended at the front counter. She pulled a bag from a shelf under the register and gave Gina a sneer.

Gina curled a lip and turned her back.

"No charge," Dixie said, apologetically.

Lexie didn't protest. She picked up the bag and exited to a drizzling November day.

Dixie followed. "Sorry my waitress wench harassed you. That woman sure has a deep hate."

"She got Red. I think that's enough victory over me."

Dixie pulled at the two inch dangling earring trapped in her platinum bouffant hairdo. "Gina thinks that you're a threat to her marriage."

Lexie focused on the restaurant sign, "He left me and married her."

"She's afraid that you're still in his heart," Dixie explained softly.

Lexie's gaze turned to her face. "The day he married her I gave up. She'll have to get over the jealousy."

Dixie waved a finger in the air. "I wouldn't bet any money on that. Gina thinks you'll lose the election and find a job elsewhere."

"For once I agree with her—on both counts."

She squeezed Lexie's shoulder. "You eat your dinner. Time to cast my vote for you. I'll cancel out Gina's vote—happy to say."

"Every vote is appreciated."

Lexie's feet crunched the fallen leaves as she crossed to her office. A slight chill in the air didn't lessen the heat generated in her body from facing the prospect of losing her job to Slick. She'd have to deal with the search for a new job and an unknown path to the future.

She started the day by wadding her long black hair into a swirl on the top of her head. Delia, her secretary, told her to comb it out and put it into a ponytail or braid. Lexie understood the point. She looked like an unkempt loser before she actually lost the election.

She pushed the office door open. "Sorry it took so long. The devil's trio held me up: Gina, Clayton, and Slick."

Delia turned from her new computer. A scowl emphasized her lined forehead. "What did Gina say?"

"She's a snot, as usual."

Tye's dark eyes focused on his sister. "The Mayor was at the restaurant?"

"Yes, with his best buddy, Slick. He offered to buy the last dinner before my defeat."

"Those jerks, never in my sixty-three years have I known a bigger pair of fools."

Lexie smiled. Delia was more like an over protective mother than an employee.

"I'll warm our burgers in the microwave."

Delia snatched the bag, "Let me."

Lexie sank into a chair. "Every time I walk into this office, I feel like I've opened the wrong door."

"That's the only good thing about this nasty election," Tye commented. "Mayor Clayton approved the renovation so Slick would have a nice office when he defeated you."

"After years of managing with one old computer, now there are three new ones. The brown walls are now painted cream and we have a wood floor. One of the two cells walled in to make a private office for the new sheriff. Yep, with all this, he'll be mighty fired up if I win."

Tye broke in, "With all that and the new oak desks, file cabinets and leather chairs, the city is out at least twenty-five thousand dollars."

Delia handed Tye a burger. "A kick in Clayton's ass if Lexie ends up with this fancy office instead of his man."

Tye chuckled, "That's what I call justice."

The trio sat around the five-foot conference table. Their mouths gave up conversation and chewed burgers and limp fries.

Lexie's eyes rose as the door opened. Wilbur Langley walked toward the conference table. His weathered face cleanly shaven and his sparse gray hair combed to the side.

"I'm back, Sheriff Girlie. They let me out early 'cause I was a model prisoner."

"I heard there was overcrowding at the prison." Tye rolled his eyes.

Wilbur nodded, "That pushed me over the final hurtle."

Lexie pushed back her chair. "Why are you here, Wilbur?"

"Looking for my boys. Heard they were placed in foster care after their mom was murdered."

Lexie saw Tye clutch the chair arms. His features stiffened, as if turning to stone.

"Gabriel and Seth were adopted," Lexie explained. "No fathers claimed the boys."

"I couldn't claim them from a prison."

Lexie continued, "Department of Human Services followed procedures. An ad was placed in the Oklahoma City paper requesting their fathers come forward."

Wilbur's voice pitched higher and higher. "They don't deliver papers to a prison cell. Nobody told me nothin' and you all knew where I was. I want my boy back."

"Just one?" Lexie questioned.

"Only one is my flesh and blood. They can keep Seth—the Indian boy. Gabriel is coming home with me. He's all I got left."

Tye fired back, "I remember when I first saw those boys. Gabriel's little butt was covered with dried shit, and red as a fire engine. They had nothing to eat and were living in a meth lab. You left them alone. No boy deserves a father who's a sorry piece of humanity."

Wilbur's arms crossed in front of his chest. "I'll do better by my boy."

"You won't get the chance."

A vein in Wilbur's forehead throbbed. "You ain't got no say about my boy, Deputy."

"I have plenty. I legally adopted Gabriel and Seth. They're my sons now."

Wilbur howled, "You ain't gettin' away with this shit. Gabriel's my blood. I'd sooner he was dead than with a lawman."

"You come near my son, and I'll break every bone in your body. Then I'll feed the remaining mush to the buzzards."

Wilbur's mouth gaped, "You'll burn in hell for stealing my son." His anger propelled his body toward, then out, the door.

Delia clutched her hands together. "Dear God, what will that maniac do?"

Tye punched a number into his cell phone, "Jamie, where are the boys?"

"Playing in the backyard."

"Lock them in the house."

"What's going on?"

"Wilbur's out of prison. Claims Gabriel is his son. I'm afraid he'll kidnap him."

Jamie's words resounded beyond Tye's ear, "OH NO."

His words clipped out. "I'll talk to their caseworker at DHS, then head home. Have the boys play in the basement."

Tye hung up without a farewell to his wife. "I'll question Myrna before DHS closes at 5 o'clock."

Lexie and Delia's concerned gazes followed him out the door.

CHAPTER TWO

Wilbur's agitated raving assaulted Tye's ears as he walked through the double doors at the human services building.

"I want the head man. You fools gave away my boy, and you better get him back." Wilbur snapped at the check-in clerk.

Tye stood back as a man with white wavy hair, Sam Flack, approached Wilbur.

"Let's talk in the conference room, Sir."

Wilbur bellowed, "Don't want all the folks in the lobby to know you gave away my blood?" At that moment he caught sight of Tye and pointed. "To that man!"

Sam shook Tye's hand. "An opportune time for you to show-up."

"I'm not here as law enforcement. I'm here because Langley threatened my son."

Wilbur's lip curled, baring rotten teeth. "I didn't threaten nothin'. I want my stolen boy back."

"Follow me," Flack directed.

The men ended up in a long room with three tables end to end and approximately twenty chairs at the edges.

"What's the problem, Tye?" Flack inquired without emotion.

"Wilbur showed up from prison and claimed Gabriel is his son. As you know, I legally adopted Gabriel and his brother."

"Who was your caseworker?"

"Myrna."

"I'll call her."

Five minutes later a slender blonde arrived. The folder gripped in her hand shook. Her frightened blue eyes avoided Flack's face.

Sam's hand reached for the folder. "You're dismissed, Myrna. We'll discuss this later."

The director's eyes glanced quickly over each page. "An official review is required."

Wilbur glared, "I'm right, ain't I? You people screwed up and gave my boy away by mistake."

Flack leaned toward him, "We'll review the case, Mr. Langley, locally and at the state office. Call me in forty-eight hours."

"Ain't got a phone," Wilbur muttered.

"Then come back here in two days. You can go now."

Wilbur chinned toward Tye, "How 'bout that deputy? Is he leaving, too?"

Flack pulled at his ear. "Yes, both of you go. I'll figure this out."

The red that seeped into Tye's brown complexion gave the illusion of war paint. "There's nothing to figure out. Gabriel's my son."

Flack gestured for the men to leave. "I'll review the case thoroughly."

The pair exited without comment. Back on the front sidewalk, they walked their separate ways. Each man positive that he was Gabriel's father.

CHAPTER THREE

The one dim light in the sheriff's office reflected against the clock as the hands turned to midnight. Lexie stared at her cell phone, willing it to ring. The polls closed at 7 p.m. She expected news of her defeat by now. She rolled back the desk chair, stood, stretched, and then walked toward the window facing Dixie's restaurant. Loud music escaped from the front door at 6 p.m. as Slick's supporters entered. The music had stopped, but bright lights still shone from within. Most of the vehicles were gone. Clayton's Cadillac and Slick's Ford truck still occupied spaces in front of the restaurant.

Delia stayed until 9 p.m. then Lexie sent her home. Sky, Lexie's toddler, spent the night with her dad, Red. Tye went home to protect Gabriel. She'd even sent her nephew, Brody, home. He manned the phone a few nights a week when J.J. was on patrol. There wasn't a point in both of them staring at a phone half the night. Her head couldn't wrap around what might be taking so long.

She and Slick agreed to bring in outsiders to tabulate votes since the sheriff election was controversial. She feared Clayton would cheat to hand the election to Slick. But somewhere along the line, he became so confident of Slick's victory he gave in to her insistence that outsiders tabulate the votes. They both trusted

Judge Marcus Simpson, and he was asked to oversee the count.

The roar of a truck engine brought Lexie's attention back to the window. Slick's black truck sped out. The inside of the restaurant went dark. Dixie and a few others exited the front door.

It's over.

Her cell phone vibrated on the desk. She ran across the room and grabbed it.

"Yes?"

"Marcus here. Congratulations, Lexie. You won by six votes."

"Slick and Clayton will demand a recount."

Marcus' words streamed out. "Clayton already yelled for one. I told him 'no.' I supervised two recounts, and you came out the winner on all three counts. I told him he wasn't wasting any more of my time or anyone else's. You're it girl."

"Thank you for being an honest man."

"How I was raised. Going home to bed. I've got early court tomorrow. Goodbye."

A childish giggle escaped from her lips as she glanced around her newly decorated office. *Clayton will probably rip the expensive wood off the floor. Glad I've got a job, but I wonder what kind of hell fire he'll use for revenge?*

Tye's voiced sounded alert when he answered the phone.

"You still have a job, Bro!" she whooped.

"You won?"

"You sound surprised."

"Not as shocked as you, I bet."

"Sorry to wake you, but I couldn't wait."

"Glad you called. I kept one ear awake hoping I'd hear from you."

"I'm coming in at 10 a.m. tomorrow because Sky has a doctor's appointment."

"I remember."

"I'll phone Delia then head home. Bye."

Delia's "hello" sounded apprehensive.

"We won another two years!"

"Thank goodness. I wrestled my pillow waiting for your call."

"I won by a whole six votes."

"Too close for comfort," Delia yawned.

"Stop wrestling that pillow and get some sleep. See you tomorrow afternoon. Goodnight."

"Night."

Lexie thought about calling her mom. But a second later she remembered Margo always found something hateful to say, so she didn't phone.

Lexie glanced around her pretty office one last time then left with a smile on her face. She locked the door and walked toward her Jeep. Clayton's Cadillac was parked behind her.

He exited his car as she pulled the door handle on her vehicle. The streetlight highlighted the hate in his eyes. "You think you've won but you haven't. One way or another the fools, in this town, will realize that you aren't sheriff material. Sooner or later I'll get you out of Diffee."

Lexie shrugged and leaned against her car door. "I don't understand what I did to deserve all this hate."

Rage shot from his mouth, "You forgot my dead son? Not to mention your bitch mother destroyed my marriage. I think that's more than enough."

Lexie controlled her tone. "Your son took a pay off from a murderer, who later killed him. As for my mother—it takes two."

Clayton snapped, "You should've caught that man long before he killed my son. My wife didn't know about your mother until she spread gossip that I slobbered after her like a love sick pup."

"Attempting to ruin me is a waste of your energy."

"It's worth every ounce, and I have plenty more where that came from."

Lexie settled in the car seat, started the engine and didn't look back.

CHAPTER FOUR

The morning sun, peeking through her worn bedroom drapes, greeted Lexie. She felt pumped instead of tired from her night's vigil. She tossed the worn quilt to the side and rolled out of bed; ready to take on bad guys who threatened the people of Diffee.

After eating peach yogurt for breakfast, she pulled on blue jeans and a white peasant top. She didn't realize, until she was almost to Red's house, that her outfit was the same one she wore the day he proposed to her.

Her Jeep followed the familiar road to Red's three-story house. She was surprised he continued to live there, considering his father committed suicide in the barn. Logic, however, told her he didn't have the money to start over. Rumor had it that his wife, Gina, wouldn't hear of moving to a lesser property.

Lexie rang the front bell, hoping Red would answer.

The door opened wide. He held his little redheaded daughter. Her cheek pressed against his, undeniably showing that their hair was the same shade of red and their eyes a crystal blue.

"Mommy," Sky announced, and reached for Lexie.

Lexie smooched her forehead, then gathered Sky in her arms.

"How's my sweet girl?"

"Play?"

"You played with your daddy. Now it's time to visit the doctor.

Get your blankie."

She lowered her two-year-old to the floor. Sky toddled off in search of her favorite possession. Lexie leaned toward Red, "How's your world?"

"Okay. I heard you got re-elected."

"Probably a miracle," Lexie grinned.

Red cleared his throat, "Not really. Most folks respect you."

Lexie looked into his eyes—a mistake. A feeling of loss invaded her chest leaving her wordless in response to his compliment.

His words stumbled out, "I better help Sky find her blanket. He snatched her up, "Let's check upstairs little one."

Gina walked across the dining room and stopped in front of Lexie. "I saw how close you stood to my husband," she hissed.

Lexie backhanded the spit sprinkles off her left cheek. "As you know, I'm here to pick up my daughter."

"So you say, but I'm not falling for your crap. Red will dote on our baby when I get pregnant. Sky won't be special."

Lexie slowly exhaled, "You don't know your husband very well."

A low growl sounded from Gina's throat. "You bitch, I know Red better than you. Back off my husband. He'll never forgive your devious lies."

"That's his decision, not yours."

"The sound of Red's feet on the stairs shut Gina's mouth."

"Found the blanket," he looked suspiciously at his wife. His eyes glanced at Lexie then back to Gina's sour face.

"Time to go, Sky. Give your daddy goodbye kisses."

A diaper bag in one hand and Sky in the other slowed Lexie's departure long enough to hear Gina's command.

"You keep that witch out of my house. She can pick up her kid on the porch."

Lexie didn't hear a response from Red, but maybe there wasn't one.

CHAPTER FIVE

Tye glanced at the clock for the tenth time in five minutes. "When is Lexie supposed to get here?"

Delia rolled her chair to face him, "At 1 p.m., you're in a mighty big hurry to leave."

"I'll question Myrna and find out what's happening. When I phoned DHS the clerk said she wasn't at work."

Delia limped to the window and opened the blinds. "Lexie's coming up the sidewalk."

Tye stood as she entered, "Is my little niece doing okay?"

"Perfect, according to the doctor."

"I'm off to hear Myrna's take on Gabriel's case. Phone if anything comes up."

His truck engine roared as he gave the gas pedal too much pressure. The trip to Myrna's duplex was short.

He knocked repeatedly. Finally, he heard footsteps on the other side. The door opened slowly.

Myrna's pale face was streaked red. Black eyeliner had settled on the bags beneath her eyes giving the illusion she'd participated in a brawl.

"May I come in?"

"Yes," she whimpered.

Tye sat on an overstuffed flowered chair. Myrna covered

herself with a blanket on an identical chair across from him.

"Give me a heads up on Gabriel's case."

Myrna rocked back and forth: a throw pillow clutched to her belly. "After my boss took my statement he consulted the state office. They put me on leave with pay until the investigation ends. Flack told me to find another job. He said there was little chance they'd take me back after this fiasco."

"They think you screwed up?" A grimace settled on Tye's face.

"Flack said that I knew Wilbur lived with Naomi and the boys. I was also aware that Wilbur was in prison and should be contacted."

"Why didn't you?"

"No father was listed on any of Gabriel's paperwork. I didn't think a man that old could father a child."

"They can and do."

"He wasn't listed on the birth certificate. Naomi claimed she didn't know who the father was."

Tye felt sweat beads erupt on his forehead. He picked up a magazine, and fanned himself. "Didn't you consider that she might lie to get more aid?"

"Certainly a possibility. It's a crime families get more assistance if they deny a father is involved."

Tye continued to fan, "And why else didn't you check this out?"

Fast paced words spilled out, "I didn't want that drug dealing slime to have the boys. They love and trust you. I should've contacted Wilbur, but I wasn't willing to take the chance. If Wilbur hadn't been released early from prison the boys would've been teenagers when he was free. A judge would've asked them where they wanted to live."

Tye's tone hardened, "Don't share that confession with anyone else."

Her teary eyes widened. "Isn't it better if Gabriel has a real father, even if he can't live with him?"

"That doesn't take in account the transition pain he'll go through if Wilbur gets him back. The other issue is my heartbroken family."

"I'm sorry."

"I received a call early this morning to meet with Flack and Wilbur at 3 p.m. I better head out."

···•••●●•••···

Tye lumbered into the lobby at the Department of Human Services. Wilbur sat on an end chair. His body straightened, and his mouth clenched when Tye came in sight.

Tye checked in, then sat on the far side of the room. Probably fifteen people waited in the lobby including half a dozen kids in tattered clothes. All six were happily engaged in puzzles and blocks.

Sam Flack's voice beckoned from the hall. The men followed him to the conference room. Wilbur reached to pull out a chair.

"Don't bother to sit." The two men studied Sam's face and words. "Based on the information I've acquired; there were mistakes made in my agency."

"I told you so!" Wilbur jabbed.

"Our first step is to obtain DNA samples from Gabriel and Wilbur. No point in wasting the court's time if Gabriel isn't Wilbur's biological son."

A gleam radiated from Wilbur's eyes. "He's my boy. Got my nose."

Flack shook his head, "Proof is required, Wilbur."

"Works for me. Anything to show this fool deputy he must butt out of my boy's life."

"I've arranged with the hospital to take samples from you and Gabriel. You go now, Wilbur. Tye, get Gabriel tested within the next twenty-four hours."

"How long before we know the results?" Tye asked.

"Within two weeks. I told the lab tech it was a priority. You two are dismissed. There's nothing more to talk about until after we get results."

Wilbur's taunt reached Tye's ears across the parking lot. "My boy! My boy! My boy!"

A sinking dread settled in the pit of Tye's stomach. He breathed deeply in and out. *It's too soon to give up. I must hope for the best.*

He tried to shake his foreboding on the drive home. Gabriel was a bright little boy, who picked up on his dad's moods. Somehow he'd make a fake smile work this evening.

Shouts greeted him from the side yard as he opened the front gate. "Come play football, Daddy," Seth called.

"You got your big brothers. I'll help your mom with supper."

Gabriel ran and gave him a hug.

"If I knew you had that mighty hug for me: I'd have come home sooner."

"I always have a hug for you."

"And I like every one of them. Run and play with your brothers. Brody can't beat Seth and Adam without you."

The hug didn't make him feel better. It only emphasized what he might lose.

Tye swiped his feet on the kitchen doormat. "What's for supper, wife?"

Jamie leaned from the skillet of gravy to give him a peck on the cheek. "Roast, mashed potatoes, gravy, and green beans for starters, then apple pie for dessert."

"Sounds good."

"You look depressed. What happened at DHS?"

"The director admitted that DHS screwed up when Wilbur wasn't contacted. They are requiring DNA testing. Can you take Gabriel to the hospital in the morning to give his sample?"

"I have time. I assume, without proof of paternity Wilbur's case will close?"

"I think, it's a given, Wilbur will get custody if Gabriel is his biological son."

Jamie's tone heated, "The man is scum. He neglected the boys when they lived with him. Nothing could be worse for Gabriel."

"I know. Let's talk about something else. I've got to calm down before I blowup or bawl. Do you want the gravy stirred?"

"Sure. I'll mash the potatoes. Let's host Thanksgiving dinner at our house. Sad to say, it may be the last one Gabriel has with our family."

"Sounds like an explosive gathering. Your father, who despises me, and my mother with her venomous personality, are quite the pair. Then there's Delia, who had her heart broken years ago when Mom seduced her boyfriend."

Jamie continued the train of thought. "Let's not forget Delia's current man friend, Sloan, that your mom tried to seduce."

"You're a brave wife to consider having these people at the same table."

"Maybe just stupid."

Tye watched the gravy bubble up. "You said it, I didn't."

"I'll threaten my father, and you do the same with your mom. If they ever want invited back to a family gathering, they'll play nice."

"Works for me," Tye agreed.

"Holler for the boys," Jamie directed, as she set the roast beef platter on the table.

The unruly foursome barged in the back door soon after Tye's yell.

"Wash your hands," Jamie instructed. "It ruins the food's flavor to mix it with sweat and dirt."

Adam laughed, "Sounds yummy, Mom."

Jamie ruffled his hair.

The six seated around the table, Brody offered a prayer. As soon as "amen" his question hurried out. "What did you learn at DHS?"

Tye felt his previous sinking feeling return. Brody wasn't one to think about the possibility this conversation shouldn't include his little brother.

"No decision yet. They're doing DNA testing to determine if Wilbur is Gabriel's biological father."

"Do you study for a DNA test?" Gabriel asked.

Jamie smiled, "No son, that test doesn't require a book."

"What's DNA?"

Adam quipped, "Stands for Dances Not at All."

Gabriel did a little jig beside his chair. "See I can dance."

Jamie clapped, "You certainly can. You and I will talk more about DNA later."

"Okay, Mom."

Jamie looked at Brody then Adam. "Geez, now that you guys have those burr haircuts…"

Brody interrupted, "And Adam built some muscles to replace his mushy body."

"You look identical," Jamie finished.

"I'll work-out with my brothers," Seth announced. "I want muscles."

"Me too!" Gabriel sang out.

Seth's head shook vigorously. "You can't go with us. You'll live with Wilbur."

Gabriel's small body shot from the chair. His fist shook in the air. "Daddy won't let Wilbur take me." His feet pounded the floor as he ran toward the bedroom.

Jamie trotted after him.

"Seth, you hurt your brother's feelings," Tye snapped.

Seth shrugged, unsure of his crime.

Gabriel's crying filled the air as the four finished supper.

Brody pushed in his chair. "I've got to head out: church tonight."

Tye didn't think he'd ever get used to Brody turning to religion. He expected his wild boy to end up in prison, not spreading God's word. It was enough to make a man believe in miracles. Which was exactly what Tye wanted—a miracle.

CHAPTER SIX

Tye startled awake at the sound of his cell phone. He glanced at the time. His mind jumped to something Lexie frequently said. 'If a phone rings after 2 a.m. it means something terrible happened.' "Hello."

"J.J. here. Got a bad one; a guy was beat to death. Thought I'd better phone you, since Lexie has her baby tonight."

"Check in, but tell her I'm already on my way. Where to?"

"Old apartments at Elm and Fifteenth Street, number 32."

Tye rolled out of bed.

Jamie sat up and yawned, "What's going on?"

"Murder at the Elm Street Apartments, which means it's time to go to work." He leaned down and kissed her lips. "Try to get more sleep."

Tye splashed cold water on his face, then soaped his body as the shower water turned hot. He slid his arms and legs into his pressed grey uniform. Twenty minutes later he pulled up at the apartment complex.

Most of Diffee was well kept. The Elm Street Apartments weren't part of that *most*. The units were housed in four stories of mismatched stone with peeling redwood trim. Much of the human scum of the town resided in the complex. At least a dozen times a month someone from the sheriff's office was called out to handle a disturbance of some sort: noise, drinking, drugs or robbery. Murder wasn't the subject of any previous call.

Apartment 32 was an efficiency unit, at the end of a hall. It consisted of a long room with appliances on one wall, and a pull out bed on the opposite wall. The bed down, Tye sidestepped toward the bathroom and the victim.

J.J. leaned against the open bathroom door. "Come on out, Miss. There's no point in staring at a dead body."

Her words tumbled out, "I screamed for him to leave Bo alone. That crazy man circled his hands around my neck. Told me to shut up, or he'd slash my face."

Tye stuck his head in, "Who was he?"

The woman looked up from the closed toilet seat, where she sat. "He was a stranger. Sock thing pulled over his face. I told him to take our money and go."

"Did he take the money?"

"No. Said he came to beat Bo to death.

"What's your name?"

"Anna Reynolds."

"Go outside while J.J. and I search for evidence."

The woman gave a final glance toward the body. A croaking breath escaped from her throat. She pushed past Tye and disappeared out the front door.

Water covered Bo's reclining body past his nipples. Tye assumed the killer left the body soaking to wash away evidence. The water was discolored from the beating. Bo's swollen face indicated he lived through most of the ordeal. His right elbow bent inward, a bone protruded.

As they leaned the victim forward, they saw lash welts across his back. A blood-smeared belt, thrown behind the toilet, was the obvious weapon of choice for this phase of the beating.

Houser from the Oklahoma State Bureau of Investigation entered with his partner.

"Bo is in the bathtub, sir," J.J. informed. "I'm thinking it was an attempt to drown the evidence."

Houser surveyed the carnage. "Who's the wailing woman blocking the front door?"

"Victim's woman," J.J. said.

"Did she see anything?"

"The maniac forced her to watch."

Houser spouted, "We'll pull this body out, wrap it, and take it to the coroner. I'll leave a man here to collect evidence."

Tye took another look at Bo. "Easy call for the coroner: beat to death. Go door-to-door, J.J. Ask people what they heard and saw. I'll question the girlfriend."

Anna reclined against the rock side of the apartment, outside the front door. No neighbors loitered to offer solace or comfort. Tye reached out a hand. "Come, we'll talk in the patrol car."

She stood with his support, and clutched his arm as he maneuvered toward the vehicle. She squeezed her hands together and stared out the window as she sat.

"What's your name and relationship to the victim?"

"I'm Anna Reynolds. He was my boyfriend."

"Did the killer's voice sound familiar?"

"No."

"About how tall?"

"Don't know."

"Was he white, black, or Indian?"

"Too scared to notice."

What color were his eyes?"

"Her head rolled from side to side."

Tye felt the irritation rise in his gut. "Why don't you know anything?"

"He'll kill me."

"He had the opportunity and didn't take it."

"If I blab he'll find me and slaughter me like a pig. That's what he said with his hands around my neck."

"If you don't help he'll murder others. There's always a chance he'll get back to you."

"I have nothing to say."

Tye circled the patrol car and opened the passenger door. "You can't stay in the apartment until the investigation is finished."

"My purse and keys are in there."

"Go back in and point them out. Jot your cell number on this paper. I want to know where you're staying. That way I'll know where to look first when you disappear."

After retrieving Anna's belongings, Tye walked her back to the street. He noted how she visually searched the area, then got into her old Chevy truck. The engine roared and smoke puffs floated toward the sky as she peeled out.

J.J. sped toward him. "Not getting any cooperation. Anyone who bothered to answer my knock claimed they slept all night."

"I'm not surprised."

J.J's eyes scanned the area. "Where's the witness?"

"Took off like a frightened rabbit. I figure she'll crawl in a hole somewhere. Let's report back to Lexie."

CHAPTER SEVEN

Lexie lifted her second cup of coffee and took a final gulp. "Guess I should've gone to the murder site. I thought they'd be back by now."

Delia looked up from the computer. "It always takes longer than we think."

"I know. Are you and Sloan joining us for Thanksgiving dinner?"

"Only because you, Tye and your kids mean the world to me. I'll eat and run if your mom harasses me."

"I'll leave with you if her mouth starts spewing insults."

"That's not necessary. I may scratch her eyes out if she flirts with Sloan."

Lexie's brow furrowed.

"I'm kidding, girl."

Lexie pulled up the window shade and saw Tye, followed by J.J, park in the spaces out front. She opened the door.

"You two take a long time to solve a murder."

Tye rubbed his face, "I guess that's why we're only deputies."

"Sit down and tell me what you know."

Tye spoke first, "Bo Sander's woman is scared shitless. Won't give a hint about the perpetrator."

"She saw it happen?"

"An eye witness without a mouth," J.J. summarized.

Lexie tapped her pen on the desktop. "The killer threatened her?"

"Told her he'd slaughter her like a pig. She claimed the guy was a stranger."

Delia chimed in, "Which she'd say to cover the trail."

"Of course," Tye acknowledged.

"What about the apartment sweep, J.J.?"

"Done by me, and Houser's men. They got nothing, and I got the same. Apparently, no one in that apartment complex has sleeping problems, or gets up during the night to pee."

"It's a rough place," Delia contributed. "Low-lives won't help catch one of their own."

J.J removed his weapon. "Okay if I head home Sheriff? I could use a little shut eye, since I'm back in a few hours."

"Come in two hours later. Brody covers the phone. He'll call me if there are problems."

"Later."

Delia handed a folder toward Lexie. "Look who I found: Bo Sanders."

Lexie removed the note attached to the file front. She read aloud. "Case closed. Bo Sanders was exonerated from the brutal death of six-year-old Lindy Reynolds. Lindy's mother, Anna Reynolds, swore that Sanders wasn't the man who beat her child to death."

Lexie fingered through the papers looking for the autopsy report. "The girl's back was marked by deep lashes. A bone protruded out the elbow from her twisted right arm. Face was distorted from facial blows."

"Poor child," Delia sympathized.

Tye reached for the folder. "These injuries are identical to the ones I saw on Bo."

"Pull Lindy Reynold's chart, Delia," Tye directed.

"Here it is."

Lexie read, "Anna Reynolds wasn't charged with the death of

her child, Lindy. Evidence indicated that someone of greater strength and stature attacked the girl. Bo Sanders testified that Anna was with him before and after the estimated time of Lindy's death. The couple swore they returned from a movie and found Lindy dead. The babysitter, they claimed to leave the child with, was never found."

"Who was Lindy's father?" Tye queried.

Lexie's eyes scanned more pages. Her pitch hit a high note. "Barney Sims—Slick."

"Oh my," Delia shrieked. "You investigate Slick, and he'll claim its sour grapes from the election."

"I won. That's all the payback I wanted."

Delia disagreed, "That's not what Slick, Clayton and his followers will say."

"I'm thinking this better be a team interview, Sis."

"I think you're right—for a change."

Tye yanked her braid, "Smartass."

Lexie pulled her purse from the desk drawer. "Let's get it done. A dead body in a bathtub isn't enough drama for you today, Bro."

"That was early this morning. I'm getting a bit bored, or maybe I'm falling asleep."

They traveled to a back road. Dust flew as Lexie accelerated the patrol car. Finally, she spied the gate that surrounded Slick's three-story brick house. The structure was set in a forest of trees. She parked in a bare spot about half mile from the structure. The pair talked as they tramped through the trees.

"It must have cost a fortune to build this place. Getting labor, brick, and wood to the middle of nowhere is expensive," Tye stated.

"You know our theory—drug money."

"I wonder if Clayton would defend Slick if he knew Clay Jr. bought drugs from him?"

"You didn't have any proof, Tye. As I recall, you didn't know what was in the bag that Slick handed Clay Jr."

"I'd bet on it!"

"And you'd probably be right."

The six-foot gate swung open as they walked forward.

"Look on the front porch. Slick's ready to welcome us."

"He must have cameras everywhere, or he wouldn't have known to open the gate."

Slick hollered, "Ready for me to take over, Sheriff? Running scared from the murder last night?"

Tye paused at the steps. "That's why we're here, Slick. You and the victim were enemies. Does the name Bo Sanders ring a bell?"

A crooked smile tightened Slick's face. "It's been a long time since I've felt this good about anything. The truth is I hated him in every cell of my body. Wish I observed his brutal beating."

Lexie eyed the man's creepy smile. "You received information on his passing mighty quick."

"I have friends in low places. What do you want?"

"I discovered Bo was accused of beating your daughter to death."

"Bo wanted child support so Anna claimed the kid was mine. Tried to force me into a DNA test. I told them I wasn't playing their fool's game."

"Then they left you alone?" Lexie asked.

"The crazy man killed Lindy because he didn't make any cash off her."

"You know that Bo murdered the child?" Lexie questioned.

"I wasn't there, but it makes sense, doesn't it? I told him to go to hell. One of my men roughed him up. That night the kid ended up dead. I'm sure they thought I'd feel guilty for her death, but I didn't."

Tye eyeballed Slick; "You never had sex with Anna?"

"Plenty of times with her, and a hundred or so others. None of them got pregnant. Doctor told me when I was eighteen that my sperm count was low. I had a million to one chance of ever fathering a child."

Lexie saw no regret in the man's eyes. "Did you ever wonder if your one in a million baby was Lindy?"

Slick smoothed his mustache, "I didn't, and don't, think that."

"You should reconsider. I saw Lindy's photo. She looked like you. A dimple in her chin and black hair. Somewhere along the line, you realized that Bo killed your little girl. Was her photo in the Diffee newspaper? Is that when you saw the resemblance? Is that why you decided to have him killed?"

"Stupid to think I'd kill him after all this time. However, I'm sure this speculation is dramatics on your part."

Tye spoke, "Where were you between 11 p.m. and 2 a.m.?"

"In bed—alone—asleep."

"Too bad you didn't have one or two of your hundred lovers in bed with you last night," Tye countered.

Slick's jaw hardened, "I don't appreciate your harassment. When it's time to put together the proof for your impeachment proceedings, I'll throw in this murder accusation. You're here to twist the knife of my lost. That's unprofessional and a waste of taxpayer money."

Tye rubbed his chin, "If you'd taught some of your friends in low places how to read. You'd have won the election."

"Get off my property!" Slick roared.

The pair retraced their route to the cruiser, then back to the town.

Tye gave Lexie a salute as he exited the car. "I'm headed home. Jamie has chores for me in preparation for Thanksgiving dinner."

"See you then. Hope we can keep the relatives from fighting."

"No one wants that more than me."

CHAPTER EIGHT

Jamie's arm muscles strained as she lifted the turkey out of the oven, and placed the rack over a cookie sheet to catch drippings.

Tye held an electric knife. "Ready for my carving skills?"

"Nope, let it rest thirty minutes before carving."

Tye sat on a kitchen stool. "I want food on the table within ten minutes after the folks arrive."

Jamie nodded, "Let's force them to eat dinner before someone gets pissed off."

"What's my next job, wife?

"Put the butter, salt and pepper on the table."

"Where are the boys?"

"Supposedly cleaning their room."

"Sticking everything under their beds like last Christmas?" You thought it was funny, I didn't."

"I recall."

"Is this family dinner a mistake, Tye?"

He gave her lips a sudden peck. "Of course it is. We knew better than invite all our crazy relatives here at the same time."

"Next time slap me when I suggest something stupid," Jamie sighed.

Tye draped an arm over her shoulder. "You'll have to hit me

for agreeing to the stupidity. I've wished for the last two days this meal was just for you, me and our boys."

"Go ahead and carve the turkey. We'll get the relatives in the front door, sit them down, pray, and make them stuff their faces."

Tye squeezed her shoulder. "Sounds like a good plan."

Jamie called into the living room. "Brody and Adam, get in here and set the tables."

Adam leaned against the kitchen doorframe. "Why so uptight, Mom?"

"One never knows what my dad and Tye's mom will say or do to cause turmoil. I want dinner finished before someone gets mad."

A firm knock, at the front door, summoned Tye.

"Come on in." Opal, Jamie's mother, hugged Tye. Jim ignored his outstretched hand.

"I'll put these two pumpkin pies in the fridge," Opal offered.

Jim hunched in the recliner, and stared at the television screen.

Adam sat at the end of the sofa. "Who do you think will win the game, Grandpa?"

"I don't give a damn after the Sooners and Cowboys are out of it."

"I thought you liked the Razorbacks?"

Jim snarled and shook his head.

Gabriel raced to welcome Lexie, Sky, and Margo. Seth pushed past them. He met Delia and Sloan as they came up the sidewalk.

Delia and Sloan each set a dish on the table.

"Here's the sausage dressing I promised and homemade bread."

"I stole a few bites," Sloan confessed, "and it's mighty good cooking."

"What can I do, Jamie?"

" We're ready to eat. Husband, head everyone this way."

Jamie sat at one end of the table and Tye at the other. The

four boys sat around a card table, under the arch, between the living room and dining room. Margo maneuvered herself between Sloan and Jim. Delia ended up across from Sloan. Sky sat on a step stool between Lexie and Delia.

Tye glanced from one bowed face to the next as he said the Thanksgiving prayer. All eyes were closed as he spoke. He thanked God for each of them, including his shrew of a mother and belligerent father-in-law.

He wondered if the conglomeration of personalities, better known as his family, represented God's sense of humor or His plan for Tye to learn patience. A goal he'd not yet accomplished.

"I have a prayer," Gabriel offered.

"Go for it, son."

"Thank you for Daddy and Mommy. God, please don't let Wilbur take me away."

All of them joined in, "Amen."

Jim's voice spiked, "What's that boy talking about?"

"We'll discuss it later, Dad."

Margo blurted, "Is that drug dealer taking Gabriel away from you?"

Tye's eyes shot daggers. "As Jamie told Jim, we'll talk about it later."

"Well, pardon me for caring about my grandson."

"Always a mistake when you take in kids that aren't your blood," Jim spouted.

Brody grumbled, "You didn't mind giving away your blood. Have you forgotten how you forced your daughter to throw away your grandsons?"

Jim's left hand pounded the table. "Your dad was a piece-of-shit teenager. He couldn't take care of himself much less my daughter and two babies. I don't regret my decision for a second."

Brody's voice rose, "It doesn't bother you that I was raised by a madman?"

Jim's nostril's flared, "Not my fault where you ended up. You could've make the best of it instead you became a thug."

"Please everyone." Lexie pleaded, "Jamie worked hard cooking this dinner. End this conversation."

Lexie observed Jim's scowl and Brody's fisted hands, but thankfully, they shut up.

Only the clicking of silverware and the clatter of passing plates interrupted the silence for five minutes.

Margo pressed her hand over Sloan's. "Are you moving to Diffee? I'd like to know you better."

Sloan pulled his hand, but Margo grasped it tighter. Beads of sweat formed across his forehead.

Margo continued, "Not many good looking, single men, in this town. The locals already grabbed up lookers like Jim." She used her free hand to squeeze Jim's upper arm, then winked at Opal.

Jim looked pleasant for a change. "I think you're too hot to handle for us country guys."

"I remember you were quite the wrestler in high school. Surely, I wouldn't be too much of a challenge." She winked at Opal a second time. "Of course, you're tied down with Opal."

Opal's face paled. Her fork quivered as she positioned a sweet potato chunk toward her mouth.

"You see, Sloan, I'm a lonely, single woman who can't find love, or sex either for that matter. A handsome single guy—like yourself—could turn me into a happy, satisfied woman."

Sloan jerked his hand from Margo's grasp. He circled the table, pulled out Delia's chair, and dropped to one knee. "I planned to do this later, but now is the perfect time." His hand dug in his pants pocket and pulled out a tissue square. He unwrapped the paper and held a diamond ring in front of Delia's face. "I love you with all my heart. Please be my wife."

The tears that filled Delia's eyes during Margo's seduction now flowed with joy. "I love you too, Sloan. Yes, I will marry you." Delia smiled at Margo, "Maybe that will protect you from cougars."

Gabriel's face twisted with curiosity. "What cougars?"

Everyone but Margo laughed.

"Did you call me a cougar, Delia?"

"Thank your lucky stars I didn't call you something worse."

An unexpected smile stretched Margo's lips. "Something else I'm thankful for today. You know, if you waited a year you might take off twenty or thirty pounds before the wedding."

"She's perfect the way she is," Sloan defended.

"Amen to that," Tye seconded.

"I'll move to the other side of the table," Lexie offered. "You sit beside your bride-to-be."

"Have you thought about a wedding date?" Opal asked.

"I'm thinking January, in the sunshine, if it's okay with Delia. We talked about going on a cruise. What do you think about that, my dear?"

"I love the choice!"

"Then that's what we'll do."

···•••●●●•••···

Four hours later Tye and Jamie sat on the front porch swing, hand-in-hand.

"We survived my mother and your father."

"Just barely, and never again will we sit them at the same table."

"Never again," Tye repeated.

CHAPTER NINE

Early Friday morning, Lexie parked the police cruiser in front of the motel that housed Anna Reynolds. Lexie reread the notes on Bo Sanders and Lindy before exiting her vehicle.

She needed Anna to disclose information. Tye's unsuccessful attempt may have been due to her recent trauma. Maybe woman-to-woman she'd get clues out of Anna.

Lexie knocked, knocked, knocked some more, and then pounded the door. One eye peeked from the curtain's edge. Lexie held her badge toward Anna's peering eye. Something ground against the floor inside the door, then the lock clicked.

Black eye make-up streaked down Anna's face. Dried gel arranged her bangs into spikes. "What do you want?" She squeaked through a six-inch space between the door and the frame.

"I want your help." Lexie gently pushed the door.

Anna motioned to a worn chair. "I told your brother everything I knew."

"You told him nothing."

She clutched at her stiff hair. "If you saw what I saw, sister, you wouldn't talk either. I was lucky to get away from that maniac. He threatened to shut me up permanently."

"Bo suffered the same injuries as Lindy. Doesn't that seem odd?"

"Never thought about it."

"I read the information from Lindy's murder. Either the killer beat both your daughter and Bo, or he was paying Bo back for her death. Bo's dead now. He can't hurt you anymore. Is he the one who murdered your child?"

Anna reclined against the headboard. "Doesn't matter: they're both dead and nothing will them back."

"He's free to hurt someone else because you won't cooperate. If Bo didn't kill Lindy, you must have. You were the ones with her."

"I loved my girl," she whimpered.

"But you loved Bo more?"

Anna picked at a bedspread hole. "He turned into a foaming mad dog because Slick refused to pay child support. After Slick's men beat Bo, he took it out on Lindy. I tried to stop him, but he went crazy. He had plans for that money. Start a new business and buy a house. Slick ruined it all."

"Slick claims that Lindy wasn't his daughter."

"I counted it out. Stayed with him two months and seven months later I had Lindy."

"No, intercourse with other men during that time period?"

Her words came out in a frantic rush. "He would've killed me. Told me he didn't share. I'd better not cheat on him if I wanted all my girl parts."

"When did you tell him about the pregnancy?"

"I never wanted him to know. I was afraid he'd take Lindy from me."

"But he didn't want her after all?"

"Denied her when it cost money."

"Did Slick kill Bo?"

Anna's gaze focused on the ever-expanding hole in the bedspread. "No."

"Was it one of Slick's men?"

"None of them that I knew."

Lexie insisted, "Describe the man who killed Bo."

"No way."

"Don't you want him to pay for murdering your lover?"

"I don't give a damn. He killed my child. He deserved death."

"Probably one of your family members thought the same and murdered Bo. Maybe you're keeping your mouth shut so someone you love won't be implicated."

"None of my kin ever lifted a finger for me, much less made the effort to hurt someone who killed my child. I didn't know the maniac."

Lexie pressed, "I won't leave this room without clues."

Tears caught in her lashes. "He'll squeeze my neck until my eyes pop out."

"You have two choices. Number one: I tell the newspaper that you refused to divulge information, and let you leave town. Number two: I tell a reporter that you spilled your guts, and I'm on the trail of the murderer."

Anna's saggy posture stiffened. "You wouldn't dare lie. You're a sheriff."

"Give me three things and I'll let you go. Less than three and I'll tell a reporter you gave me information even though you didn't."

She rested her head on one hand. "You won't tell anybody?"

"Nor will I throw you in jail for withholding evidence in Lindy's case. I'll say you took off scared—a waste of tax payer money to hunt you down."

Anna looked at the door. "I'd like to get out of Oklahoma."

"That's what I want for you—a new beginning. Three clues then start a new life."

She held up fingers, "Three things?"

"Three things," Lexie repeated.

Anna's hand swiped across her face. "His skin was dark."

"African American?" Lexie clarified.

"Indian."

"Go on," Lexie prompted.

"He wore a metal cross."

"What else?" Lexie said softly.

"I know he was over six feet tall, 'cause he was taller than Bo."

"You're doing well. Describe his face."

The finger manipulating the bedspread hole ripped a six-inch gash. "I can count," she huffed, "and that was three. When do I leave?"

Lexie's hand grasped the doorknob. "I'll purchase you a five hundred dollar prepaid credit card. That's all I can take from my designated funds without informing the mayor's office. While I'm doing that, get packed. I'll return in thirty minutes. We'll stop at Bo's apartment for your other belongings. I'll drive you to Fayetteville, and put you on a bus."

Her legs swung off the bed. "I'll get ready."

Lexie eyed the surroundings as she left: nothing out of the ordinary. The sooner Anna was out of Diffee the better. Hearing the perpetrator was a tall Indian did nothing to solve her case. Diffee's Native American population was close to fifty percent.

Lexie glanced at her watch. A wave of foreboding swept through her body. It was 9 a.m. The time designated for Judge Marcus Simpson to announce the results of Gabriel's DNA test.

CHAPTER TEN

Gabriel buried his face in Tye's side as they sat on the wood bench in the courtroom. Jamie held Gabriel's hand. Tears fought to erupt, and ruin her façade of confidence. Brody and Adam sat on either side of their parents. Seth was spared this time of mental torture.

At Jamie's urging, they packed Gabriel's clothes and toys in the car trunk. Tye refused at first. Claiming the action meant there was no hope. Jamie's logic that the boy wouldn't have anything from home if they lost custody finally convinced her husband. Adam and Brody kept their little brother occupied, tossing the football in the backyard, while the parents snuck belongings in the trunk.

Wilbur paused at the end of the aisle. "Howdy son, been a long time."

Gabriel's eyes rose to Wilbur's weathered face, then his gaze fell to his own small hands that twisted on his lap.

Wilbur smiled at Tye, "My day has finally come."

Tye firmed the grip on his shivering son.

Wilbur slid into the bench across from them.

The judge didn't look at either father as he read his statement. "DNA testing has confirmed that Gabriel is the biological child of Wilbur Langley."

Wilbur's smug faced turned toward Tye. "Told you so, asshole."

"MR. LANGLEY, such behavior and language aren't tolerated in my courtroom."

"Sorry, Judge."

Simpson continued reading. "An investigation of the proceedings that facilitated the adoption of Gabriel Langley to Tye Wolfe found that errors in the process resulted in the violation of Mr. Langley's rights. Due to these errors, the adoption of Gabriel isn't legal, and parental rights are returned to his biological father."

"No!" Gabriel cried out. "Please, Mr. Judge, let me go home with Daddy and Mommy."

Simpson's face softened, but his words held firm. "I can't change the law, child. You were illegally adopted."

"That's for damn sure." Wilbur cursed under his breath.

Simpson massaged his forehead. "The court apologizes to Mr. Langley for these government agency errors."

Wilbur waved an accusatory finger. "You're apologizing so I won't sue. It won't work. Your government screw up caused me pain and suffering. Somebody will pay."

"Threatening me, Langley? Let me return the favor. You so much as get a speeding ticket with Gabriel in your car, or if I find out he's not in school every day, I'll put him in foster care with Tye Wolfe. I'm waiting and watching for you to make a mistake. If you show up in this court on drug charges; I'll send you to jail for the rest of your life."

Wilbur's harsh tone diminished to a low simmer. "I'll do right by my boy, Judge."

"You better. The third weekend of each month Gabriel will have visitation with his brother Seth at the home of Tye Wolfe. This court is adjourned."

Tye leaned over and whispered in Gabriel's ear. "I'm always here. You're forever my son."

Gabriel's arms wrapped around Tye. "Daddy, please no."

Wilbur stood at the end of the bench. "Come on, boy, let's go home."

Tye placed a hand on each shoulder as he faced Gabriel. "You're a warrior. Do you know where you are, son?"

Gabriel patted his chest, "In your heart, Daddy."

"Yes, always. Wilbur is ready."

Gabriel stood straight with chin raised. Small fingers flickered toward his brothers.

Jamie kissed him on the forehead. "For your first visit, I'll cook fried chicken and we'll play Crazy Eights."

Gabriel looked at the floor in front of Wilbur. "I'm ready."

"We have a few of his toys and clothes in my car trunk," Jamie offered

"Never you mind, woman. I won't take handouts from you child thieves. Follow me, boy."

Tye, Jamie and the twins exited the courthouse. Myrna stood outside the door. They stopped beside her.

Tears streaked her pale face. "They fired me. Maybe that will make you feel better. I'm so sorry. Please forgive me. I wanted the boys in a good home."

Brody patted her back.

"Myrna, I agree with what you said before. Better for Gabriel to be with us even for a short time. He is forever my son. I forgive you." Tye took Jamie's hand and moved toward the car.

Tye's eyes rose heavenward. Two birds circled overhead then dove to the pavement and pecked a dead possum—road kill. A perfect sight for the way he felt. Pressure formed a knot in his chest. Wilbur took his heart, but he'd get it back—one way or another.

CHAPTER ELEVEN

Jamie ran out her front door soon after Lexie honked.

"She must've looked out the window." Delia speculated from the front passenger seat.

Lexie sighed, "If she feels anything like I do, she's in a hurry to have a girl day."

"Me too!" Delia's giggle wasn't unlike a five-year-old girl.

Jamie settled into the back seat. "Take off, before my guys realize I'm gone."

"Lexie's glad to get away, too."

Lexie steered the Jeep toward the highway. "Last few days were drudgery with Bo's unsolved murder, and Clayton breathing down my neck.

"I hope my wedding shopping isn't keeping you from something important."

"Delia, my dear, you're the only person that's important today."

"For sure," Jamie agreed. "Your wedding cruise leaves on December 31st. That only leaves nineteen days to get your trousseau ready."

Delia formed a finger steeple in the air. "My, oh my, the wedding is coming fast. Don't know if I can get everything finished."

"You're not alone. We're a dynamic, wedding planning trio. We'll get it done."

Delia's tone turned serious. "There's something private I need to discuss."

Lexie felt hairs prickle on the back of her neck.

A nervous laugh floated from the back seat. "Let me out at the next light, if this is a sex talk."

Delia's skin flushed a lovely pink. "Mercy, I wasn't talking about that stuff. My man is a mighty fine teacher."

"TMI," Lexie grinned.

Delia's head cocked toward Lexie. "What does TMI mean?"

Jamie interpreted, "Too much information."

"Now I've forgotten what I wanted to ask you goofy girls."

"Something private," Lexie reminded.

"Ah yes, I'm thinking about dying my hair to my natural brunette before the wedding."

"Go for it," Jamie whooped from the back seat.

"What if Sloan doesn't like my new do?"

Lexie glanced at Delia's hair. "Your hair has as much brunette as gray. I can't imagine Sloan will care."

A sneaky grin turned up the corners of her lips. "I'll do it and blame you two if Sloan doesn't like my new color and cut."

"You brought us along as scapegoats," Jamie accused.

Delia shrugged her shoulders, "Works for me."

After an hour drive, Lexie found a parking space in front of Best Bridal. "A good omen: easy to load all of Delia's finery."

Delia whispered near Lexie's ear as they entered. "I'm afraid that skinny young girl won't know how to dress an old fat bride."

"Hush that negative talk or you can't have wine with lunch," Lexie warned.

Delia's body straightened and she held her chin up in a snob imitation.

"May I help you?" Skinny Girl asked.

"Yes, young lady, I've waited over sixty years to be a bride, and I'm here to buy my finery."

"Cool. What color dress?"

Delia sat on a white velvet chair. A sign plastered above it said *Bride's Throne*. "I haven't decided on a color. Show me everything you have in size sixteen."

Skinny Girl stammered, "Are you okay with mother-of-the-bride clothes?"

Lexie reminded, "We have a dozen other shops we can check if you don't find the perfect dress here."

"We'll shop until we drop," Jamie contributed.

Skinny Girl returned with a mauve suit, a navy suit, and a beige suit.

"Assistants, do you like the suits?"

"Hell no," Jamie barked.

"No way," Lexie shook her head. "I forbid you—no suit on your wedding day."

"Too uptight," Jamie added. "Look for something flowing with a little sparkle."

"Oh my," Delia protested. "I'm not the foo-foo type."

"You're a first time bride. You won't look like a princess in a suit." Lexie directed Skinny Girl, "Look for dresses and skirt sets."

The sales girl returned with three selections. "These are all we have in your size."

One dress was fitted white satin with a fake diamond belt. Another had pink ruffles from under the breasts to the floor. The third outfit was a pale blue skirt with a sparkling over-blouse of the same shade.

"It's beautiful," Delia sighed.

"Try it on," Lexie ordered.

Delia swirled as she stepped out of the dressing room, then posed with a hand on her hip. "What do you think, girls?"

Lexie and Jamie chimed in unison, "Beautiful."

Skinny Girl echoed the same.

Delia admired her reflection in the mirror. "I love it! This is the dress for me."

"Matching shoes?" Skinny Girl asked.

"Yes," Delia answered. "I'd also like a short veil. Do you think that's okay, Lexie?"

"I think it's a good idea."

Two hours later the trio sat in a restaurant sipping red wine while they waited for steaks.

Jamie frowned, "Delia, I'm sorry, but...."

"Your sad face makes me mighty nervous."

Jamie stumbled over words. "I hate to disappoint you, but Seth and I can't go on the cruise."

Delia didn't respond.

"Too much time off from teaching, and Seth struggles at school. I can't risk him getting further behind. The main reason, however, is Gabriel. He's lost weight and looks depressed. I can't bear to miss visits."

Delia squeezed Jamie's hand. "Is Wilbur treating him badly?"

"No outward signs of abuse, but his spirit is deflated. He's not the happy little boy he was with us."

"I understand. Your boys must come first. It's sad that little Gabriel is having a tough time."

"The waitress returned and served their meals. "Anything else?"

Jamie cut into the meat, "Steak looks perfect."

"More wine, ladies?"

"Not for me," Lexie answered, "but top off their drinks. If they get drunk I'll hear good stories."

Jamie lifted her empty goblet toward the waitress. "I'll risk spilling my guts."

"Me too," Delia seconded.

Jamie took a sip, "What have you learned about cruise weddings?"

"Everything," Delia answered. "We bought a small event package. It included the ceremony, flowers, champagne and a photographer. We show up and get hitched."

Jamie sawed into the well-done steak. "Are you getting married on an island?"

"We decided we'd get married on the ship—New Years Day."

"That's the way to start a new year," Lexie exclaimed.

"Perfect for tax purposes."

Lexie touched Delia's cheek. "My lady is always tracking the paperwork."

"That's my job," she chirped.

"And you do it very well."

Jamie reiterated the plans. "Let me get this straight. You're getting on the cruise ship December 31st, and married on January 1st."

Delia's cheeks blushed, "Better to start the honeymoon as soon as possible."

Lexie held up a goblet, "I'll toast that!"

····•••●●●•••····

At day's end, Lexie toted wedding finery to Delia's bedroom. After all the purchases were spread on the bed, Lexie reached for a final hug.

Delia's misty eyes met Lexie's gaze. "This was one of the happiest days of my life. Thank you."

"Jamie and I enjoyed your bachelorette fun day as much as you. See you Monday."

Delia's moist cheek touched Lexie's face as her arms wrapped firmly around her. "You're my favorite girl."

"And you're my favorite lady."

CHAPTER TWELVE

Two weeks had passed since Tye lost custody of Gabriel. Lexie couldn't bear to look at his face. The hopelessness in his eyes and slump in his posture conveyed his pain.

Tye sat on the edge of her desk. "What are you doing today, Sis?"

"Thought I'd take Flame for a ride toward Wilbur's house. You can't go there, but I can."

"I'd appreciate it. Tell Gabriel that I love him. We're ready to celebrate Christmas with him."

"I will. By the way, there's nothing new on our murder case. Dead end—pardon the pun."

"I'll reread the notes and try to find an angle."

"Good plan. I'll get back with you after I see Gabriel."

"Give my boy a big hug."

"For sure."

···•••●●●•••···

Gravel shot into the air as Lexie parked her Jeep and attached horse trailer behind Lulu's Country Store and Diner. Flame whinnied in protest of the bumpy ride.

Lulu pulled Lexie's shoulders forward and smooched her forehead. "Let me fetch dumplings for my sweet girl."

"I'll eat when I get back. I owe Wilbur a visit."

"I bet I know why. That scum bag with that dear little boy ain't right."

"Have you seen them in your restaurant? How was he treating Gabriel?"

"Treated him okay. Boy looked forlorn. His usual ornery smile was gone."

"Was he clean?"

"In new blue jeans and a cowboy shirt. Looked good."

"In a way, I hate to hear that. If you're ever concerned, call me."

"You know I will. Don't you worry, Lexie girl. Wilbur won't keep up his good daddy routine. He'll return to his low-life self."

"I hope that happens soon. Tye, Jamie and Seth are lost without the little guy."

"You go about your business, girl. I'll save a bowl of dumplings."

"Sounds good."

Lexie saddled Flame, then led him to a dirt area before she mounted.

"Sorry, it's been so long Flame, but I know the stable guy takes you out every day."

Flame's head reared back and a whinny sounded. Lexie thought it meant that a stranger wasn't as good as riding with her. She held the reins loose, and Flame took the lead. Occasionally, she pulled the reins to adjust the direction.

She loved the forest in the spring and summer, but the deadness of winter had settled in. The leaves crunched beneath Flame's hoofs. The bare tree branches intertwined making a wood tapestry across the sky. The creek remained still. Its flow stopped by a dry autumn. Now the creek's only chance to fill its banks was an abundance of winter snow.

It took over an hour to reach Wilbur's shack in the woods. The tree camouflaged site, a perfect hiding place for a meth lab. How fortunate if he was cooking meth today.

A few yards from the house she halted. A fancy red and black four-wheeler set beside Wilbur's front porch.

She slid from Flame's back and tied him to a tree limb.

She stalked up the steps and listened by the door. It crashed open. Fearful she'd fall backward; her hands grabbed the screen as it swung forward.

Slick Sims stood in front of her; his face screwed in disgust. "What the hell, Wolfe? Why are you here?"

"I wondered the same thing about you, Slick. Looking for a new drug partner? Wilbur has vast experience. Or perhaps you threatened him out of your territory?"

"Wilbur's gone out of business."

"Worked out well for you—no competition."

"Get some proof, Sheriff, or shut up. I've heard enough accusations." Slick gave her shoulder a slight push as he passed.

"Aunt Lexie," Gabriel ran into her arms.

"How's my best boy?"

"Okay," he murmured.

Her arms wrapped around and squeezed. "That's from your daddy. He loves and misses you."

Wilbur tugged at Gabriel's arm. "Get in the house, boy."

Gabriel's red-rimmed eyes filled with tears.

Wilbur's leathery features formed into hate. "Why are you spying on me?"

"I came to visit my nephew."

"You've seen him—now go. I know what you're up to, but it ain't goin' work. I'm good to my boy, and you'll never prove otherwise."

"Your history negates your words. Friends like Slick aren't a positive testimony to your changed man routine."

"Slick ain't my friend," he snarled.

"Were you warned to stay out of his drug business?"

"I ain't got knowledge of Slick's business. Get out of here or I'll ask the judge for a restraining order."

"That's not necessary. I'm on my way."

Lexie saw a small hand waving from a side window. She threw Gabriel a kiss and mouthed, *I love you.*

CHAPTER THIRTEEN

Lexie punched in a phone number as soon as she arrived in her office.

Tye's words rushed, "How was Gabriel? Did you tell him I missed him?"

"He looked subdued, and sad. I gave him a giant hug from you."

"Do you think Wilbur is treating him right?"

"He's attempting. Gabriel wore new clothes. I saw a few toys in the yard. I also saw Slick at Wilbur's shack."

"That's disturbing. Did you get a feel for why he was there?"

"No, and Wilbur denied any connection with him."

"Of course he would."

"I'm working night shift. Brody is off with Myrna. J.J. called in sick."

"Okay, Sis, I'll relieve you in the morning."

Lexie buried her nose in Sander's case notes. No eureka moment: this time or the six times before.

Sky was spending the night with Red, and his shrew wife. Lexie's gut ached after she left her toddler. Red promised he'd stay home all night. She knew he'd never let any physical harm come to Sky. Regardless, Gina's hateful mouth anywhere near Sky was a concern.

The phone rang at straight up midnight. The voice grumbled, "I'm getting real tired of Diffee."

"What's up, Houser?"

"We got a call on a bizarre case in your county."

"Define bizarre?"

"Come and see for yourself. Elm Street Apartments—again."

"Don't I get a hint?"

"Better to see for yourself: room 217."

Lexie splashed water on her face hoping to bring out the appearance of alertness.

When she arrived, at the apartment complex, she noted the four state vehicles in a line. *I wonder why it took so long for them to call me.*

Houser met her on the steps.

"Why am I the last one here?" She blurted.

"I called J.J. I knew he worked night shift. Figured he was busy since there wasn't a response."

"What's the secret, Houser?"

"Someone cut off the guy's penis: a bloody mess. Every man in the place grabbed his balls to make sure they were still hanging."

"You know the victim's name?"

"Latest alias is Rocky Coffman. Found drug paraphilia, empty liquor bottles, and child porn on the computer. He's a pedophile: long record and recently out of jail."

"He won't hurt children anymore."

"That's for damn sure!"

Lexie's attention focused on the bloody spot that surrounded the victim's lower body. *Wonder if he lived long enough to make the connection between the evil he'd done and the evil done him.* "Any helpful evidence?"

"Not yet. Guy has defensive wounds. Maybe the killer left something behind on Rocky's body."

"I'll research Rocky at my office. Phone if you find anything."

"Will do. By the way, Mayor Clayton sent a message, through my supervisor, to notify him whenever there's a major crime in your county."

"That jerk. What was your response?"

"I'd follow his orders as soon as he earned his badge."

"Thanks."

"Glad to stick it to a politician any chance I get. You must've pissed him off."

"I beat his buddy in the election. He's out to get me."

"Now I understand."

"Tell your computer guy to send Rocky's porn file to me. I'd bet my bank account that a parent of one of his victims paid him back."

"That's the logical conclusion. I'll stay in touch."

Driving back she concentrated on the penis-less pervert. Something she'd never say aloud, but having this guy out of circulation was for the best.

About 3 a.m. the file from Houser arrived on her computer. She studied Coffman's record. He served two terms: A three-year prison stay for photographing a naked four-year-old girl, and an additional eight years for molesting a seven-year-old.

She jotted down the girls' names and the names of their families. One family was from Arkansas and the other child from Texas. *Rocky moved around: Difficult for a victim's family member to track him*

The last record she found noted Illinois as his state of residence. Interesting that he lived in Diffee prior to the arrest in Texas. She pulled the photos up on her computer. If she found a Diffee child, she'd have suspects close to home.

Lexie's chest ached as she looked at the beautiful little girls. At first, the photos were taken around the lake. Mostly little girls in bikinis, but there was one of a woman changing a diaper. Her eyes watered as she viewed page after page.

Her hand clicked to the next photo. Lexie's tired eyes strained as she enlarged the photo. Lindy sat in ruffled panties on the steps of the Elm Street Apartments. The next page showed her naked on an old recliner. Lexie recognized the chair as the one she saw earlier in Rocky's apartment.

Nausea churned Lexie's stomach and forced her to the toilet. *The horrors Lindy faced in her short life were unbearable.*

Lexie heard the office door rattle as she splashed water on her face and flattened down her helter-skelter hair.

"It's 7 a.m., Tye. Why are you early?"

"To give you some relief. You look like death warmed over."

"Another murder—brutal."

"Diffee goes years at a time without a murder and now we have two."

"Yes, right after Slick lost the election."

Tye lowered into a chair. "You think there's a connection?"

"I've thought about that the last couple of hours. Slick was connected to Lindy, who was connected to both victims."

Tye's forehead wrinkled. "You think Slick's having people killed to discredit you?"

Lexie tapped the desktop. "That's what I wonder. It sounds ridiculous when I say it out loud."

""It's farfetched."

"Think about it. Both murdered men hurt Slick's daughter. To him they're disposable people. People would agree that they got what they deserved. He can pay the victims back for hurting his daughter and prove me incompetent as a bonus."

"I guess it's a possibility, or maybe you're paranoid."

"Funny, Bro. Clayton sent a message through Houser's supervisor that he wanted a heads up when a major crime occurred in Diffee."

"That adds credibility to your theory. I bet Houser said 'screw him.'"

"This is one time I appreciated his bad attitude. Got to get some sleep before I pick up Sky this afternoon. I'm out of here.

CHAPTER FOURTEEN

Tye's heart rhythm increased as the words assaulted his ears.

"This is Principal Bradford. Trey Moore is dead." His shaky voice uttered the message.

Tye shook his head in an attempt to clear the shock from his brain. He focused on the caller's report.

"When Trey didn't show up for his bus route this morning, I looked for him." Bradford paused.

"Go on, Principal," Tye prompted.

"Trey's wife Doris, sat on his front porch with a rifle on her lap, blood spots on her clothes, and pale as a ghost. She's still sitting like a zombie.

"I'll be right there."

"Hurry. I'm afraid she may shoot one or both of us."

Tye's foot pushed the gas pedal as he activated the siren. He called the Highway Patrol as he sped toward Trey's farm.

He respected Trey for his volunteer work with kids. He was a suspect in the Wendy Elliot murder. Tye discovered, during his investigation, that the man wasn't a murderer. The death of Trey's son was an accident that nearly destroyed his life. A life he recovered through volunteer work.

The porch swing rocked slowly back and forth. Trey's widow sat still, except for the slight foot motion that kept the swing moving. Tye didn't know the woman. His only knowledge of Doris was Delia's comment months before that she'd forgiven Trey for the accidental death of their son. Trey shot his son when they were deer hunting. He convinced Doris that he wasn't drunk at the time. Tye wondered if she ever forgave the man.

Tye tensed, "Doris, hand me the rifle."

Gray-streaked hair snarled around her face. Her wild eyes jerked from Tye to the rifle and back. "It belongs to the devil. He controls it. First it killed my boy, now it killed my husband."

Tye's insistence was gentle but firm. "Doris, you must give me the rifle." His hand reached toward her.

"Don't touch evil."

"Where's Trey's body?" Tye directed the question to Bradford.

"Out in the woods—under a tree. The one with a hunting stand built into the branches."

"Doris, did you shoot Trey?"

She pinched her cheek. "I thought I forgave him for killing Alan."

"Your son?"

"My dear boy. We could've lived happy ever after, but Trey ruined our fairytale. I'm sad now and forever."

Tye slipped on gloves and grasp the rifle.

She held the weapon tightly against her body. "You can't have it."

"It's evidence."

"It's evil. The devil controls it."

Tye touched her shoulder. "Don't listen to the devil." He jerked the rifle from her grasp. "The principal called an ambulance to transport you to the hospital. You aren't well."

She shivered, "What about Trey's funeral?"

"The funeral home will prepare Trey for his final resting place."

Her voice sounded dead and distant. "I don't feel like pressing Trey's suit today."

Houser and company arrived as the ambulance pulled into the clearing.

"No, I can't go. Trey will think I deserted him because he shot our boy. Doris stared at her hands while moving them in front of her face. Is this Trey's blood? Did I hurt him?"

"Where are we taking this woman?" The ambulance attendant asked.

Houser answered, "Behavioral Health Unit at the closest Tulsa Hospital. One of my guys will accompany you. She's not a danger to anyone but herself."

Tye walked with Houser toward the tree stand.

"One shot did it," Houser summarized. "These country women shoot rifles as well as their men folk."

Tye moved a few yards from the tree. "Grass flattened, she aimed from here."

"Hole in his back, so she snuck up and fired. Poor guy didn't know what was coming. Don't piss off your wife is the moral of Trey's story."

"I'll try to remember your sage advice. Are you married, Houser?"

"No. Any woman interested in me is blind, deaf, and stupid to boot. I'm not marriage material."

Tye didn't restrain his laugh.

"We've done all we can do here—clear-cut case. They'll do a psyche evaluation on the woman, then decide what happens next. I'll make sure all the lab results come back to you, Tye."

"How long do you think?"

"They usually do thirty days inpatient and come up with a diagnosis. I bet murder one is off the table due to her son's traumatic death."

"Thanks, Houser, you and your men can head out. I'll wait for the coroner to finish and body transport."

"That works. I don't want to see your face anytime soon," Houser quipped.

CHAPTER FIFTEEN

Lexie woke with a jolt. She rolled from bed and trotted to the front door. Pulling back the window curtain she caught a glimpse of Gina's sour face. Sky wailed beside her.

Lexie swung the door open and gathered Sky in her arms. Her words sizzled out, "What's going on, Gina? Sky's frightened."

"Good lord, she's a baby. She doesn't feel scared. Take your bawling brat and teach her manners. She's spoiled rotten, doesn't mind, and won't stay out of things. My kid won't get away with that crap."

"Babies who don't explore are abnormal. That's how toddlers learn."

"One, don't preach at me. Two, I'm not your babysitter while you laze around all day."

"I'm sure Red told you that I worked all night. Where is he? He volunteered to watch her until 3 p.m."

"He was called out on a job. A rich oil guy paid double for a trip to Vegas." Gina's nostrils flared and her chin lifted. "By the way, Red and I are expecting a baby. Your little game of 'baby mama' to keep my husband close won't work anymore."

"Thanks for dropping Sky off." Lexie slammed the door.

Sky whimpered as Lexie rocked. She smoothed red curls and cuddled her toddler. Sky fisted a strand of her mom's hair and wound it around her finger. Lexie turned Sky to face her. "We must wrap presents and put up our Christmas tree."

"Tee," Sky mimicked.

"It's on the front porch. I bought it when you visited your daddy."

Lexie eased Sky to the floor. "You hold the door open."

She carried the four-foot pine and stood it in the corner.

Sky's face puckered, "House—tee?"

"I know it's confusing. You don't remember last year. Your daddy decorated with us. He danced with you around the tree. I'll turn on Christmas music."

Lexie climbed the stepstool and pulled a box of ornaments from the closet. The boom box played *Rudolph* in the background.

After straightening the tree and putting on two strands of lights she handed Sky one ornament at a time. Sky's contributions resulted in a conglomeration of decorations around the tree's bottom. Lexie added gold globes to the upper section, then lifted Sky, who placed the angel at the top.

"Pretty," Sky said.

"You did a good job."

Sky snatched a snowman ornament off the tree.

"We'll have an early Christmas with Gabriel this weekend. Let's get the presents wrapped."

A tug from Lexie, and the Santa wrap rolled across the carpet. Sky flopped in the middle of the wrap. Lexie made another selection.

Sky ripped, wadded, then laughed as she dislodged the tape her mom stuck on her thumb. After a few minutes Sky quieted. Lexie found her asleep under the Christmas tree. "You're my perfect present, little daughter."

Without Sky's assistance she finished the wrapping in record time.

A rap at the door halted cleanup.

Red's face glared through the screen door.

Lexie stepped onto the porch. "Sky's asleep in the living

room. Let's talk here."

His tone stung, "Why did you get Sky? I told you I'd bring her between 3 p.m. and 5 p.m."

"Gina brought Sky home. Said she was tired of babysitting. I'm afraid she's mean to Sky."

"Sounds like an excuse to withhold my daughter from me."

"Your wife dropped her off."

"Her story doesn't match yours. Gina said you were belligerent because I wasn't taking care of Sky and you took her home."

"That isn't true."

Red's attitude darkened. "Considering your history, you're the last person I'd trust to tell the truth."

Lexie's pulse quickened, "I've taken on a load of guilt since your father died. Blamed myself for his death and you leaving me. One day recently, I asked myself why I beat myself up over a murderer. I'm tired of your hatred. My actions were nothing compared to the murder your father committed, and how it impacted my life."

Red's words spit out, "Perhaps, it blows up your ego to pretend that you weren't devious."

"I'll confess to devious, but not that I deserved condemnation for the rest of my life."

His face muscles tightened. "Forgiveness is something I'll never consider in relation to your actions."

Words spewed from Lexie's lips. "I don't want Sky alone with Gina. She thinks you'll forget our daughter when your new baby is born."

"You know better than that."

"I do, but your wife thinks you'll dump your firstborn."

"You're crazy if you think I'll side with you against Gina."

"I want what's best for Sky."

"You think I don't?" He grumbled.

"I think you're blind to Gina's motives and attitude."

"Butt out, Lexie."

"I'm telling you, I won't leave Sky at your house if you're not there. If you leave for work, call me. I'll come get her."

"If I don't?" He challenged.

"Then I'll take you to court. I won't allow the witch to emotionally abuse my child."

"Be careful with your threats. Have you forgotten how you purposely kept her from me? How your job put her life in danger? I know a judge or two who'll give me custody because of your betrayals."

Lexie forced words out: calm and flat. "I'm hoping, if you think there's even a small chance Gina is lying that you'll protect Sky. Surely her wellbeing overrides your hatred."

"Sky is the most important person in my life. I'd never risk her happiness."

"That's what I thought, but I needed to hear the words."

"I better head home."

"Come in for a minute. Look at Sky's bed."

Red grinned ear-to-ear when he saw his daughter stretched out on the tree skirt covered by Santa gift wrap. "I know who decorated the tree."

"I'll see improvement when she gets taller, I hope."

Her cell phone played its tune. A sharp voice pierced into her ear. She pushed the speaker button.

"Is my husband there?"

"He just left," Lexie lied. "He was fighting mad because you told him I picked Sky up early."

"Now he knows you're an interfering bitch."

"Even though it's based on your lies?"

"Men don't know what's good for them. You're a sick virus that he must get over. I know you want him, but he's mine. Since I'm pregnant you don't have a prayer of getting him back."

"By the way, you'll be happy to know that he believed you. You got away with your lies. Also, he threatened to sue me for custody of Sky. If he wins the court battle you'll have her night and day."

"You don't have to worry about that. I won't let him. No way am I taking care of your little brat." The phone went dead.

Red turned his ashen face as he reached the door. "I'll bring Sky back to you, or Delia, or Jamie, if I'm called to work."

"Thank you."

I wonder if he'll confront Gina about what he heard. I doubt it. He won't jeopardize his relationship with a pregnant wife.

Lexie lay beside Sky on the carpet. Soon her body succumbed to the long night and emotional afternoon.

CHAPTER SIXTEEN

Delia cocked her head toward Tye. "What are all those papers? Can't see your desk."

"Reviewing our two murder cases. Lexie has a ridiculous theory. Unfortunately, they're frequently correct."

"What's her theory?"

"That Slick Sims arranged the murders of Bo and Rocky."

"I don't understand."

"Slick has personal connections with both dead men."

"Does Slick think he can get away with murder because Lexie won't arrest him?"

"Between you and me, I think the election made her paranoid. I will say, however, Slick would get rid of two people he hated, and make Lexie look incompetent."

"Geez, your sister does come up with some weird motives." Delia's eyes flickered as the door squealed open.

Mayor Clayton tromped across the room. An icy sheen on his hat matched his cold tone. "Where's your sister?"

"She worked the night shift—off today."

"I'm aware of her foolery. The public is scared. Soon they'll demand a competent sheriff. When that happens I'll have no recourse but to replace her."

Tye's fists gripped at his sides. "Replace her with Slick? The prime suspect in these killings."

"You've gone too far."

Tye's words shot out like bullets. "Both murdered men are connected to Slick. Men he'd pay someone to kill to make Lexie look bad."

"That's insane."

"Facts are facts, Clayton, whether you like them or not. By the way, next time you visit your best buddy, ask where your dead son purchased his drugs."

Clayton's face blazed, "My son died because your sister is incompetent."

"Dream on fool."

Clayton sped toward the door. The cold wind rushed in as he exited.

Tye jogged across the room and pulled the door shut.

Delia gave him, *the look.*

"I know. I know. Lexie will bust a gut when she hears I spilled all her suspicions. My temper couldn't let it pass. He's such a self-righteous asshole."

"Clayton slammed his Cadillac door like a wild man." Brody announced as he followed J.J. in the door.

"Your dad got his dander way up," Delia explained. "My work day is over. See you tomorrow."

Brody said, "Bye" then grilled Tye. "What happened, Dad?"

"I opened my big mouth. I told Clayton his man, Slick, is a suspect in the murders. Murders he's discrediting Lexie for not solving."

Brody stretched, "Don't be sorry for calling a snake a snake."

"No proof and he'll put Slick on alert."

Brody continued, "He knows the victims?"

"It's all superficial evidence. He wouldn't get his hands dirty, which means we're looking for someone he hired."

"Someone who's long gone," J.J. assumed.

"Probably."

"Doesn't it look obvious when he kills people he hates?" J.J.

asked.

"It's not general knowledge that Slick has any connection to Bo or Rocky."

Brody piped in, "Sounds like a good deal. Kill a couple of guys you hate, in order to get a sheriff you despise fired, then you get her job. Sounds like a win-win for Slick."

Tye's voice strained, "There was another murder in Diffee this morning. It doesn't look like it'll impact us. Pretty straightforward case: Trey Moore died, the high school bus driver. I told you about him when I investigated Wendy Elliot's case."

Brody spoke up, "The drunk who shot his son?"

"It was an accident."

"You don't know," Brody jabbed. "You weren't there."

Tye blinked hard, "He was a good guy who worked with kids."

"That doesn't prove him innocent."

J.J. intervened in the father-son sparring. "What killed the guy?"

"Hunting rifle blast to Trey's back, courtesy of his wife."

"She admitted killing him?"

Tye eyed Brody, "She blamed the devil, but blood specks on her clothes and the rifle in her hands said otherwise. Houser hauled her to a psyche ward in Tulsa."

"So she's crazy," Brody concluded.

"Mentally ill," Tye corrected. "Losing her son and knowing Trey caused his death ate at her all these years. It apparently became too much to bear."

"Sad deal," J.J. commented.

"I'm out of here, guys. Brody, don't forget Gabriel's visit this weekend. We'll have an early Christmas. Plan on spending Saturday night at the house."

"When you getting him?"

"I'm picking him up after school tomorrow. I'll have something to look forward to after my brow beating from Lexie."

"You might be able to take her in a fight, old man."

"It's her sharp tongue that worries me."

CHAPTER SEVENTEEN

When Lexie arrived at work Tuesday morning, she couldn't decipher the smirk on Delia's face. "What does your expression mean?"

Delia zipped her lips. "Better if the story comes from the source."

"Who's the source?"

"I'm sure he'll arrive soon."

As if on cue, Tye came through the door. His sheepish expression further confused Lexie.

"Delia, Have you told her?"

"Not my story to tell. I'll get breakfast." Delia draped purse straps on her shoulder and limped, as fast as possible, out the door."

Lexie's eyes narrowed as she concentrated on Tye's guilty expression. "What's this about?"

"First, let me say I'm sorry."

"Already an apology. That's ominous."

"I shot off my mouth and told Clayton that we suspected Slick in the recent killings. To add to my avalanche, I accused Clay Jr. of dealing drugs with Slick."

Lexie's front teeth gnawed her bottom lip. "That was speculation and wishful thinking on my part. Now we can't investigate Slick secretly. Clayton has probably told Slick already. What were you thinking?" The pencil broke in Lexie's grip. "Since you weren't thinking, don't bother to answer."

Tye's face reddened. "I couldn't handle Clayton defending that asshole. He thinks Slick is a victim when he's actually a drug dealing murderer."

Lexie startled when the door banged open. "Speak of the devil," she muttered.

"Sheriff Wolfe, I hear you think I'm a murderer who's trying to discredit you. I'm actually your sacrificial lamb."

"Your name and sacrificial lamb in the same sentence is ridiculous."

"Here's my theory. You, or a family member, arranged the deaths and implicated me. Get rid of your adversary and become a heroine for saving the citizens of Diffee."

"Your theory is as far left field as mine is in right field. They're foolish speculation on both our parts. My brother made an attempt to support me when your comrade, Clayton, threatened my job. I'm sure your family would do the same for you."

"That doesn't sound like an apology."

"Consider my reasoning, Slick. Rocky's porn collection included photos of your beautiful little daughter. Bo Sanders beat Lindy to death. You've got cause to want both men dead."

"You keep ignoring the fact, Sheriff, that Lindy isn't my daughter."

"Anna left a lock of Lindy's baby hair. Give me a snip of yours to compare the DNA, then we'll both know for sure."

"A cold day in hell before that happens."

"I figured as much. Guess we don't have anything else to discuss. I do wonder why an innocent man refuses to have his DNA tested. It might eliminate your motive for murdering Bo and Rocky."

Slick made threats on his way out. "Sooner not later, you'll pay for your accusations and my tarnished reputation."

Lexie plucked her purse from a drawer. "I'm going to

Cherokee Marshal Service: to give them heads up that our killer is likely Native American."

"Sorry, Sis."

She left without accepting the apology. Maybe tomorrow or the next day the fire in her gut would burn out.

···•••●●•••···

The door to the Marshal's service felt extra heavy, perhaps because she didn't want to open it.

Marshal Prather, a guy who adored her in high school, turned into an enemy. Her mother's acid tongue informed a teenage Larry that he wasn't good enough for her daughter. The only positive part of this visit was the opportunity to look at his co-worker, Marshal Farmer.

Unfortunately, it was Prather who loitered in the lobby.

"Is Gus Farmer on duty?" she inquired.

"I'm not good enough?" Prather challenged. "Just like high school?"

"Don't confuse me with my mother. She's the one who said that crap. I had nothing to do with it. But you're right about one thing. I don't want to consult with you. That chip on your shoulder is obnoxious and mighty old."

Prather's body stiffened and turned toward the clerk. "Sheriff Wolfe wants Farmer." He didn't turn back even though her "thank you" sounded pleasant, at least to her own ears.

Gus Farmer circled his desk as she entered. The man was shades of brown from his dark hair, to his caramel eyes, to the earth tones of Cherokee flesh. His hand squeezed her upper arm.

Lexie felt her face flush.

"You okay, Lexie?"

"Sorry, not feeling well today. Feels like a cold coming on. I'll try not to breathe on you." *Sometimes a white lie can ward off the embarrassment of the truth.*

"I doubt you dropped by for a social visit. What's up?"

"I received a confidential report that the guy who beat Bo Sanders to death was Native American. I dropped by to inform you."

"I appreciate the warning. I bet you'll find my new case interesting."

"Someone I know?" Lexie coughed convincingly.

"You remember the Chadwick Hawk case?"

"The guy murdered by an arrow to the heart?"

"That's him. Leroy Grass, my number one suspect, was found dead" Gus pointed a finger. "Guess the cause of death."

Lexie touched her chest, "An arrow to the heart."

"Right on."

"His judgment came outside of court."

"Lexie, do you think Leroy killed Hawk."

"The day I interviewed Leroy, he denied murdering my father, but didn't deny killing Hawk. Leroy said Hawk deserved punishment. My gut said he did it, but no evidence came out during our conversation."

"Well, he may have received his just reward."

"Take an ace shot to shoot an arrow through Leroy's heart, "Lexie concluded."

"Not a hobby archer. He's likely Native American and an expert. Our people shoot to kill game, not hit the middle of a circle."

"True," Lexie confirmed.

"Anything else on Sander's killer?"

"Over six feet tall and wears a cross."

"That only leaves a few thousand suspects."

Lexie pointed, "Including you, and a few of my relatives. Thanks for making my challenge clear."

"Most of my career is based on finding Indian men over six feet tall. Good luck," he winked.

She stood, "I better continue the search. If I run into a crossover with the Marshal service I'll let you know."

"I appreciate it."

CHAPTER EIGHTEEN

Tye's face lit in anticipation as he watched Gabriel jog down the school steps.

Gabriel's darting glance fell on Tye's white Avalanche.

He slid from the seat and sprinted toward him. His arms caught him in a wide swing. A kiss landed square on his boy's lips. "My little son, I've missed you more than a polar bear misses a block of ice."

Gabriel giggled, "I've missed you more than a turkey misses his gobble."

Tye landed him on the ground. "Come on, son, before your mom comes looking for us. She's so excited she might…"

"Pee her pants," Gabriel finished.

Tye pinched his cheek. "I hope that doesn't happen, but we better get home fast."

Gabriel fastened his seatbelt. " Buckle up, Daddy."

"Yes, sir," Tye pulled the belt snug.

"What are you learning in school?"

"Nothing."

Tye ruffled his hair, "Then I'll have all the teachers and principal fired.

Gabriel's lips puckered, "Thanks, Daddy."

Tye shook his finger. "You're my little comedian. You're

always messing with my brain."

"It's fun, Daddy.... I mean Tye."

"I'm Daddy to you."

"Wilbur said he'd better not hear me call you daddy ever again. He'd find the biggest switch in the forest and beat my little ass."

"He can't hear you here."

"I'm afraid of his big switch."

"Has he hurt you?"

"No. He squeezes his face and yells ugly words."

"Let's not think about Wilbur this weekend. I still want to hear what you're learning at the new school."

"Addition, subtraction and some spelling words with six letters."

"That all sounds useful. Look who's on the front porch. Your mom is wadding her apron front. A sign she's waited long enough."

Gabriel hightailed out the door to Jamie's arms. A few seconds later he gave brother Seth a shoulder bump. The pair disappeared into their room.

Jamie smoothed the apron front. "Is he okay?"

"Looks pale. Maybe lost a little weight."

"Dark circles under his eyes," Jamie added.

"None of that is valid reason to take Wilbur back to court," Tye lamented.

Jamie set the table. "Are Adam and Brody coming for super?"

"Both are working tonight. They promised early arrivals tomorrow."

"Husband, will you get the ornaments from the attic while I finish supper?"

"Sure."

"Did you remember that Seth's Christmas program is tonight?"

"You said he plays Rudolph."

"Glad you listened."

"Not every day a man's son puts on a red nose and dances around. Thank goodness."

Tye stood in the boy's doorway, "Come on guys, I'll hand the decorations down to you."

Jamie called them to supper. "Leave the ornaments guys. Let's eat and get to school, before 6:30."

Gabriel wiggled his nose. "No reindeers allowed at the table."

Seth waved his fist.

Jamie answered solemnly, "Since it's the Christmas season, we'll make an exception."

"When will we decorate the tree?" Gabriel sang out.

"As soon as we get home from the school play," Jamie informed.

"Even if it's midnight?"

"Yes, little son, even if it's the middle of the night. We'll sprinkle you with cold water." Tye felt the ache in his chest subside as the dullness in Gabriel's eyes was replaced by a sunny, joking spirit.

····•••●●●•••····

Tye flipped on the lights that lit the trim on the house and the seven-foot Christmas tree. His brain replayed the activities from the night before, and the joy on the faces of his sons.

The family celebrated Seth's great betrayal of Rudolph at Dixie's restaurant. Four chocolate sundaes and a short drive later; the four sang Christmas songs as they decorated the tree. Finally, the boys flung silver icicles onto the tree. No bedtime complaints, from either boy.

Tye's concentration returned to the present as he sliced the ham smoked for dinner. Jamie spooned sweet potatoes, and macaroni and cheese, in bowls.

CHAPTER NINETEEN

Lexie held Sky's hand as they joined the Christmas party.

Gabriel hugged Sky, "Aunt Lexie, what took so long?"

"Sky is a slow walker."

"Don't blame her cause you're pokey. You can carry her."

"That's true. Guys get the presents from my car. Put them under the tree, please. I hope you like red long-johns."

Seth's head swayed back and forth. "Not for me."

"Do it fast, sons, while we put the meal on the table," Tye ordered.

Sloan stepped back when Margo fingered the buttons on his shirtfront.

"Hey Mom," Lexie intervened. "Arrange the packages for me."

"Surely you can handle putting boxes under a tree," Margo snapped.

Lexie whispered near her ear. "I prefer to handle your inappropriate behavior."

"Well, I never!"

"You did and you are," Lexie hissed. "Get off Sloan before Delia comes back. Don't screw up Christmas like you did Thanksgiving."

"Sloan snatched Sky to his riding knee. Tell this old horsey to giddy-up."

Sky swatted Sloan's leg, and rode the pretend pony.

"Whoopee," Sloan called.

"Whoopee," Sky mimicked.

"Come and get it," Delia called from the dining room entry.

·····●●●●●●·····

The main course consumed, Lexie forked a bite of apple pie and moved it toward her mouth. The bite halted in the air as she answered the cell phone, "Hello."

J.J.'s voice waffled, "Sorry to bother you. There's something you need to know."

"I'll move to a different room. So much Christmas excitement that I can't hear."

Tye's eyes tracked as she disappeared into the master bedroom.

"What's up, J.J.? Are you still there?"

"I'm not sure how to tell you."

"Tell me what?"

Tye entered and shut the door.

"One of Wilbur's relatives found him dead this morning. Someone cut out his tongue. His cousin called the OSBI. The guy accused Tye of murder."

"Houser investigating?"

"Yes. Mayor told him you and yours aren't to get near this case. Houser said Clayton planned to hang you both for this death."

"That's no surprise."

"Houser told me not to phone, but he isn't my boss."

"Sounds like there's nothing they'd allow me to do."

"True."

"Thanks for calling. Keep me informed."

"Yes, Boss."

Tye studied Lexie's face.

"What is it, Sis?"

"You're the prime suspect in the murder of Wilbur Langley."

"Wilbur is dead?"

Lexie noted a touch of surprise in his tone. "Not only dead, but tongue-less. Someone wanted him permanently silent."

"Are you leading the investigation?"

"Clayton made it clear that this case is off limits for both of us."

"What happened to innocent until proven guilty?"

"Doesn't apply when Slick and Clayton have the perfect opportunity to ruin us. Clayton's coming after us with all he's got. Did you kill Wilbur?" Her next words rushed, "Never mind, I don't want to know. Houser can worry about suspects. Let's celebrate Christmas. The kids are probably driving the adults nuts."

Tye didn't say a word. No quick denial. No surprised joy. A blank face with foreboding eyes was the only hints of what he felt inside. *What have you done, brother? No point in killing a man to have your son, when you'll go to prison.*

All eyes settled on the pair when they entered the living room. "Work stuff," Lexie explained. "We better get these presents unwrapped before kids climb the wall and knock down the tree."

"We're just excited, Aunt Lexie." Seth said matter-of-factly.

Tye sat on the floor beside Gabriel. "Adam and Brody, hand out the gifts."

"Me first," Gabriel begged.

Sky's little face scrunched as she stomped a foot. "My presents."

Laughter erupted.

CHAPTER TWENTY

Tye dropped Gabriel off at school Monday morning with a promise to pick him up after class. He drove toward his office with the activities from the day before repeating in his head. He told Gabriel about Wilbur's death. Seth shouted 'yea.' Gabriel spoke softly, 'I get to stay with you, Daddy?'

'I don't know what the judge will decide, son.'

Gabriel fought back tears. 'Where will they take me?'

Tye went over his response. 'They think I killed Wilbur. I didn't, but until they figure out who did, they may not let me have custody.'

Lexie reached the phone toward him as soon as he entered the office.

"Tye Wolfe here. I dropped him off at school, Judge."

"The mayor is raising hell. Said a killer shouldn't have custody of his victim's son. I can't disagree."

"I didn't murder Wilbur. Considered it, might have eventually done it, but someone got to him first."

"This is a disaster. You're a person of interest in Wilbur's murder. I can't give you custody of Gabriel."

"Think about Gabriel stuck in foster care for who knows how long."

"I can't control that. A DHS placement coordinator will pick him up after school, and take him to a foster home."

"When may we visit?"

"I'll work something out for Jamie and Seth. You stay out of the picture."

"My son needs me."

"He'll do without you until you're cleared. Assuming you're not guilty. Got to get to court."

Tye didn't say goodbye.

Lexie stopped in front of his desk. "What's up?"

"Judge says that I can't have custody of Gabriel or even visit him until my innocence is proven. So much for innocent until proven guilty."

"Are you innocent?" She asked calmly.

"You think I killed Wilbur?"

"Sounded convincing when you told Judge Simpson you didn't."

"Insulting that my sister thinks I'm a killer."

"I think you'd do anything to save Gabriel from life with a drug dealer."

"That's a valid point, but I decided to give Wilbur time to screw up on his own. A lifetime criminal doesn't suddenly become an altar boy."

"Someone besides you wanted Wilbur dead."

"I wished him gone, not dead."

"This is one case we don't have to investigate. We'll stay away—as far as possible. It'll look bad if we start messing with the evidence."

Tye pointed toward the cell. "So I sit around and wait until they lock me in there?"

"Houser will figure out what happened."

"I guess he's about to start, because here he is." Tye stated.

"I'll have to hire extra men to clean up all the Wolfe shit," Houser complained.

"Good morning to you, Houser."

"There's nothing good about this day, Sheriff."

"Your mayor yakked to my boss, who is now nipping at my ass to prove your brother is a murderer. Soon as I find a shred of evidence I'll lock Tye up and get them off my back."

""You'll put my brother in jail because people are annoying you? Interesting perspective on case solving."

"I thought we were friends, Houser. You're mighty eager to cage me."

"I'll tell you what I told your mayor and my supervisor. I've got no friends, no prejudices, and no time to deal with petty assumptions. Everyone back off and let me solve this case."

"Sounds good to me," Lexie confirmed.

Houser pointed at Tye. "You better not have committed this murder. If so, I'll find a way to accidently shoot you so I won't have to deal with the aftermath."

"Why don't you prove me innocent?"

"So far it'd be easier to shoot you." Houser looked toward the door. "Oh no, here comes the pain in my ass."

Clayton glared at Houser, then Tye, then and Lexie. "What's going on, detective? Having chitchat with your buddies?"

Houser's chest buffed. "I'm attempting to investigate a case without prejudice, but your big nose keeps sticking in my business. Hell, if Tye's the killer, it'll be thrown out because of your manipulation of the investigating officer. Not ethical to pressure me to arrest Tye when there's no proof—yet."

"Well, I never."

"You sure as hell have. What do you want now? Are you here to harass these people?"

"I'm here to tell them to stay out of this case."

Lexie placed her face six inches from Clayton's. "Don't tell me what to do. You remember my theory, don't you? The one where Slick kills people to make my department look incompetent? Here's a third case that Slick benefits from the death of the victim."

Tye joined in the attack. "Wilbur was in the drug business before he went to prison—Slick's current business. Competition for your good friend."

Lexie continued, "A little something else for you to consider. A few days ago when I visited Gabriel, your pal was harassing, the now dead, Wilbur."

"Speculation is all you got, woman."

"You're right, no proof, but I have no doubt who did away with Bo Sanders, Rocky Coffman, and Wilbur Langley. I bet Slick hired the first two done, but I bet he enjoyed cutting out Wilbur's tongue."

"Houser, close these two lunatics down." Clayton fled out the door.

"That's your theory, Lexie? Slick's responsible for three murders?"

"He was connected to all three men. He had reason to want them dead. Discrediting me is a bonus that might result in him becoming sheriff."

"You got nothing."

"That sums it up," Lexie agreed.

Houser retrieved a pen and notepad from his pocket.

"Where were you Friday evening between 7 p.m. and 10 p.m., Wolfe?"

"That was the time of death?" Lexie inquired.

"You think it was when I took my ballet lesson?"

"You in a tutu puts an interesting picture in my head."

"Cute," Houser retorted.

"Six p.m. I ate dinner with Jamie and the boys. Seven to 8:30 p.m. we were at the elementary school watching Seth in the Christmas program with a couple hundred Diffee residents. Nine p.m. we were at Dixie's having chocolate sundaes. After that we went home and decorated the tree and the boys went to bed. I put together the boys' new bikes between 11 p.m. and 1 a.m."

"That sounds rehearsed. Your wife is your witness?"

"Not the only one. My activities covered the estimated time of death. You know I didn't have time to ride a four wheeler or horse to Wilbur's place, kill him and get back."

"You didn't mention Adam and Brody during your alibi. I'm thinking one of them killed off Wilbur to comfort their sad daddy and little brother."

"They both worked Friday night. Leave them the hell out of this case."

"I'm not leaving anyone out, Wolfe. Write down the names of folks who spoke to you at the program. Also, anyone who visited with you at the restaurant."

"Don't drag my wife into this."

"Already did, interviewed her at the high school. Surely, you didn't think I was stupid enough to leave her out."

"Pardon me, murder accusations screw my thinking process," Tye scoffed

"One more thing, then I'm gone. Give me spit for my DNA sample. I want to know if you were in Wilbur's house."

Tye obliged. "Lexie and I did a drug bust there years ago, and I haven't returned. I'm confident it'll come out clean."

"We'll see about that," Houser grunted. "If I don't arrest you within three days it'll mean I don't have enough evidence to charge you. Don't want to see either of you anytime soon." Houser kicked the door before he opened it.

Lexie sank back in her chair. "Feels like a bulldozer came through the office."

"And I got crushed," Tye added.

Lexie nodded, "That's correct."

CHAPTER TWENTY-ONE

Lexie reached for the ringing phone. "I was getting worried. Why haven't you signed out, J.J?"

"Called to a murder site."

"Where?"

"Behind Clyde's bar at 4th and Oak."

"I'll be right there."

Tye looked up from cleaning his gun. "What happened?"

"Another murder."

"Do you want me to come with?"

"You take care of business here." Lexie grabbed a cup of coffee and gloves. She glanced at a note scrawled on her desk pad. It said a pedestrian was run over in an adjoining county. She stuck the message in her right top drawer, then jogged toward the cruiser. Leaves scattered across the landscape propelled by an aggressive wind. No color remained outside, only winter's biting cold.

A green truck parked in front of the bar and J.J.'s vehicle were the only signs of occupants when she arrived. She circled the bar while eyeing the Clyde's Southern Comfort sign that remained lit.

The two men stood on either side of a dead body. The corpse was dressed in a white shirt, loosened tie, shined shoes and a navy suit. His short hair was spiked from dried blood that surrounded a broken liquor bottle wedged in his head.

"You know this guy, Clyde?" J.J. questioned.

"Comes in most weekday evenings around 6 p.m. One drink then he takes off."

"His name?"

"Evan Walkin. He works this county for an insurance company."

"Did he argue with anyone in the bar?"

Clyde shook his head. "He's always pleasant. Stays to himself."

"How long did he stay last night?" Lexie asked.

"Howdy, Sheriff. Didn't hear you sneak up."

"Hi, Clyde."

"He left around 7 p.m."

"Alone?"

Clyde rubbed his whiskered chin, "Yes, as usual."

"Did anyone follow him?"

"Wasn't paying attention."

"Did you notice him talking to anyone?" J.J. probed.

"Not a soul. He sat, drank, paid his bill and left."

J.J. thought aloud, "Someone must have called him out back."

"Evan always parked in the back. I figured he had a woman at home who didn't want him in a bar. I found him this morning when I pulled in by the back door."

J.J. scratched his head. "Why didn't you find him last night?"

"I park in the front after dark. Creepy coming out the back door when I have cash."

"We'll have a good idea when he died after the autopsy results come back," Lexie noted. "What time did you get here?"

"Around 7:00 a.m. then immediately called J.J."

"What time did you leave last night?"

"Little after midnight and there wasn't anyone around."

"You can go home J.J. Get some sleep before your next shift."

"Yes, Boss."

Lexie heard him direct the Oklahoma State Bureau of Investigation officers as he rounded the beer joint.

"Damn it, Lexie. I can't get anything done for running to your rural murders."

Lexie jabbed back, "It's not like we're killing people because we love to see you."

Houser's words boomeranged from his crabby face. "I'm so lovable it could happen."

"No comment. You sure came fast."

"Worked a hit-and-run a few miles from here."

"I've got a man killed by a liquor bottle to the head."

"That's simple enough. I'll have my men gather evidence."

Lexie's gloved hand slid Evan's wallet out of his back pocket. "And I'll notify his next of kin. Maybe a family member will know why someone wanted Evan dead."

"Stay in touch," she mumbled to Houser as she skimmed through the contents of Evan's wallet.

He grumbled, "Don't I always."

She stopped at the office to track down Evan's next of kin.

Tye looked up from paperwork. "What happened, Sis?"

"Man murdered in back of Clyde's bar."

"Who?"

"Evan Walkin. Have you heard of him? According to his driver's license, he's fifty."

"Don't know him," Tye responded.

"I know the name," Delia interjected. "Years ago his teenage girlfriend died in a car crash. He was driving drunk. Accused of manslaughter but he wasn't convicted."

"Why not?" Tye wondered.

"I guess the jury took pity on him. Young kid out celebrating high school graduation. His folks moved right after the trial. Some folks harassed Evan. Most people thought he got away with murder."

"Interesting," Lexie remarked. "A drunk driver killed with a liquor bottle."

"Is that what they call poetic justice?" Tye joked.

"Nothing poetic about it," Delia countered.

Lexie crosschecked the information on Evan's license and

eventually discovered the address was current.

"I'm taking off to see if anyone is at Evan's house. Tye, check to see if Houser has any news on the case."

The siblings exited together.

Lexie put the address in the GPS. The drive gave her plenty of time to think. *Is it a coincidence the victim was killed by a liquor bottle?* She assumed that the person who killed Evan did so to avenge the teen girl's death.

She thought about asking the Tulsa Police Department to contact Evan's relatives. However, she gave up that idea for the opportunity to watch Evan's wife, assuming he had a wife, react to the terrible news. If the wife was involved, perhaps facial expressions and body language will give her away. The down side—a truly grieving person offered little logic.

Lexie climbed the stairwell to the second floor of the building. The number falling off the front door and the peeled paint, were clues to Walkin's life. A few knocks later a woman, likely in her forties, answered the door.

"Are you related to Evan Walkin?"

"He's my husband. We're working on paying our debts, but it'll take a while. What company sent the law after us?"

"None."

The woman's face squished into apprehension. "I don't understand."

Lexie softened her tone. "Evan was found dead this morning—murdered."

The wife stammered, "Oh my God."

Lexie wondered if the woman's containment was the result of shyness or being alienated from her husband.

"What did they take? His ring? His money?"

"It wasn't a robbery."

Her words rushed out, "There's no other reason. He's nearly a saint. Always helping others, putting others first—even before me."

"What did you think when he didn't come home last night?"

"He works six counties and sometimes spends nights in

motels to cut down his drive time. He called me around 7 p.m. Told me everything was fine and he'd drive home tonight. You're mistaken. He'll arrive soon. No one would harm Evan."

"Give me his parent's address so I can inform them of his death."

"She moved toward the bedroom, then returned with an address sprawled across the front of a furniture advertisement."

"They'll straighten this out," she promised.

Lexie put the address in her GPS and drove the short distance. She wondered about Evan's wife. Something about her wasn't right.

The couple raked leaves as she pulled into their driveway. Mr. Walkin meandered toward her as she opened the car door. The lady of the house leaned on a rake.

"What can I do for you, officer?"

"May we go inside? I have questions about your son, Evan."

The man moved toward the door. Lexie followed with the woman taking up the rear.

Seated in the immaculate room of yellow flowered drapes with a matching sofa and loveseat, Lexie felt like she was dropped in a flower garden.

The man leaned forward in his recliner. "We're Gene and Lila."

"I'm Sheriff Lexie Wolfe from Diffee."

"I've tried to forget that town," Lila whimpered.

"I'm sorry to inform you that Evan was found dead this morning in Diffee. An apparent murder."

Gene's hands covered his face.

"May he rest in peace," Lila whispered.

"Your son had no peace?"

Gene uncovered his face. "Not since that girl died—April was her name."

Lila continued, "He was burdened with guilt, and didn't allow himself to have a family or do anything enjoyable."

"But he has a wife."

"He married Margaret so she'd have a home. After a brain

injury from a ladder fall, she couldn't take care of herself."

"Did your son mention any contact from April's family?"

Lila responded, "The first year they stalked him. April's brother beat Evan three times. Our family moved to get away from them."

"Did Evan say if the brother threatened to kill him?"

"They all hated him." Lila's breath caught. "Evan understood because he hated himself."

"Do you think someone in April's family killed him after all these years?"

"I have no doubt," Gene answered.

"Mr. Walkin, I'm surprised your son goes near Diffee considering the bad memories, and the chance of running into haters."

"Diffee is one of six counties in his region. He didn't have a choice if he wanted his job."

"What's the name of April's family?"

"Cortland."

"Can you think of anyone else who wanted to hurt your son?"

Gene squeezed out, "No. He spent his life trying to make up for that girl's death. A good man, who made a bad mistake as a boy, and paid the rest of his life. I'm sure he's happy to move out of this life."

"I'm sorry for your loss. I'll keep you informed of progress in your son's case."

Lexie pondered her conversations with the three family members while she drove back to Diffee. None of them broke into tears. None of them wailed about the lost life. They accepted death as the best thing for Evan. She'd never seen anything like it. The strangeness of their reactions didn't leave her thoughts. She considered that one of the three took him out of his misery.

Delia waved a faded folder when Lexie walked in the office. "Look what I found."

"Evan Walkin's folder?"

"Still haven't found Evan's. She handed the papers to Lexie. "It's a case file on April Cortland's brother, John. Jailed three times for terrorizing Evan."

Lexie sat down at Tye's desk. "According to this, the Cortland family lived near County Line Road. I wonder if they're still there?"

Delia shook her head, "I have no idea."

"I'll hunt the Cortland's down. Maybe I'll get lucky and the killer will confess.

"No such luck," Delia predicted.

····•••●●•···

Lexie searched for the name on mailboxes as she drove over rocky terrain. *The family must go elsewhere to buy groceries and participate in activities.* She'd never heard the name in Diffee.

The wooden gate, beside the Cortland mailbox, fell to the ground when she released the latch. She realized the hinges rusted out and disconnected from the wood years before. A collie stood by the front steps. A low growl parted his lips.

A hunched over man with a cane in each hand rounded the corner. "Hush, Lassie. It's that girl sheriff."

Lexie stopped mid-stride,"Mr. Cortland?"

"Ernie," he corrected.

"Do you live here by yourself?"

"Yep, me and Lassie. What's the problem, Sheriff?"

Lexie's pitch rose, "Evan Walkin was found murdered this morning. Rumor has it your family hated him enough to kill him."

Ernie walked toward a fenced in area. "Here's my family."

Lexie entered the family cemetery. April's marker was in the middle. "Who are these other two people, Ernie?"

"My wife, Lottie, and my son, John. Lottie died 'cause of gangrene in her foot. John died in a car crash."

"Do you have other family?"

"Everybody's dead and buried 'cept for me. Even if I wanted Evan dead, my old truck wouldn't get me there."

"How do you get food?"

"Mostly grow my own, but a neighbor shops for me once a month."

"Do you know anyone else who felt strongly about April's

death?"

"Citizens were up in arms thirty-two years ago when it happened. They soon went on with their lives. Me and mine never did. My wife finished her life in sorrow and my son consumed by hate."

"How about you, Ernie?"

"I kept going. No choice. I admit I thought about killing the boy out of fear my son would murder him and spend the rest of his life in prison."

"Why didn't you?"

"I was a preacher at the time. Didn't think God would approve."

"Thanks for talking with me. Come by my office if you ever get into Diffee."

"I'll do that, Sheriff."

Lexie slid into the cruiser's seat then pulled out her cell phone. Delia answered on the first ring, as usual. "I'm picking up my little one then driving home. Any news?"

"Nothing new here."

"Okay, I'll see you in the morning."

CHAPTER TWENTY-TWO

Delia's bun dropped from the top of her head to the nape of her neck as she searched the W folders for the tenth time.

Lexie studied Delia's furrowed brow. "Why are you in frantic mode?"

"Because I am," she snapped. "I've searched since yesterday for Walkin's folder. It still hasn't shown up. I even walked to the courthouse and checked the basement storage. How could it vanish?"

"Tye and I will recheck. Don't be late for your doctor appointment."

"I don't misplace files. I'll keep looking."

"You're the most efficient person I've ever known. I order you to go to the doctor. It's bound to show up."

"Maybe different eyes will see it faster."

Lexie wandered the room. She finally landed in Delia's office chair and unrolled the newspaper. "FOUR UNSOLVED MURDERS" the headline read.

The subtitle was "Where's Our Sheriff?" The mayor was quoted as saying that Sheriff Wolfe should be kicked out of office. Her incompetence put the Diffee citizens at risk. "Best to stay inside," he warned. "It's not safe outside with the current sheriff responsible for safety." He also expressed his disappointment with the Diffee citizens who re-elected her.

She rolled the paper into a tube and waved it at Tye. "The Mayor is getting revenge."

"I read it. Hoped you'd miss that story."

"If Slick wasn't behind the first three killings, we may have four different murderers to apprehend."

"Do you doubt Slick's guilt?"

"We must figure out if Evan fits into the Slick theory. Delia couldn't find Walkin's old folder. Help me look. It may give us clues as to who wanted him dead, and if Slick has any connection to April's family."

Tye started with the last half of the alphabet and Lexie with A. Two hours later, still no folder.

"Let's check every drawer in the place," Lexie suggested. "Maybe Delia pulled the chart then forgot she left it in one of our desks."

"Not in mine," Tye reported.

Lexie scavenged through her desk drawers. Her gaze caught on a phone message. She read aloud, "Sheriff in Adair County reported a vehicular homicide. The man killed served prison time for a hit-and-run death."

Tye pulled Walkin's folder from under a pile of sports magazines in a side desk.

"Here it is."

Lexie rubbed the back of her neck. "Why's an old case stuck in Brody and J.J.'s desk?"

Tye rolled his eyes, "Strange."

Lexie reached out a hand, "Pass it over." Her eyes scanned the description of the charges against Evan. "His teen girlfriend was killed when he drove drunk after their senior prom."

Lexie felt the color drain from her face.

"What is it, Sis? You look like a ghost spooked you."

"An eye for an eye."

"What are you talking about?"

"All the deaths have a common thread. Each person was murdered by the method he used that resulted in someone else's trauma."

"Damn, I get it. The porn guy lost his penis and the child abuser beat to death."

Lexie continued, "The drunk driver killed by a liquor bottle. I'm not sure where Wilbur's tongue fits."

"Someone might have overdosed from one of his meth sales."

"There were at least two more deaths. Leroy's arrow to the heart, and the hit-and-run were both out of our jurisdiction. I was so sure Slick killed the first three, I missed the pattern."

"Someone is playing judge, jury, and God."

"Exactly," Lexie agreed. "The killer knew enough about Lindy's case that he inflicted identical injuries on the perpetrator."

"You think someone accessed our files?"

"Perhaps someone who forgot to file Walkin's folder back."

Tye's jaw dropped, "Do you think Brody or J.J. killed these people?"

She coughed out the lump in her throat. "I don't know what to think. I do know they're the two who have easy access to records in the middle of the night."

The room fell silent at the clatter of Brody's arrival for work. Only the sound of a branch scraping the outside window interrupted the quiet.

Brody looked from his aunt to dad. "You two sure act weird."

"We're trying to find a killer." Lexie waved a folder in the air. "Why was Walkin's chart in the bottom drawer of your desk?"

"Hell, if I know. That's J.J's desk, not mine. I sit at Dad's desk during my shift."

"Tye leveled out the bite in his tone. "Couple weeks ago when I mentioned Rocky Coffman was dead, and tied to Lindy's death, you mentioned the porn photos of Lindy. How did you know about the pictures?"

"Probably overheard in the office."

"Never discussed with you present."

"You think your memory is that good Daddy-o?"

"I'm sure it is."

"I'd rather not say."

"Speak up, Brody." Lexie commanded. "This looks bad."

Brody's fist pounded the wall. "Here we go again. Neither of you will ever let me live down my past. I killed a man who abused and raped me. I've joined church. I wanted to make you proud. Now you're accusing me of murder. You'll never trust me, no matter how hard I try."

Lexie screeched, "How did you know about Lindy?"

"Myrna told me. Lindy was her client before DHS fired her."

"She breached confidentiality to discuss this child's case with you?" Tye confirmed.

"Not like they can fire her again."

"State can still prosecute her," Lexie informed.

"Knowing you two, you'll tattle to satisfy your ever present righteous indignation. I'm leaving. You two can work my shift and find someone else to blame. Apparently, your sharp investigative minds haven't remembered the strangers in this office when it was redecorated. Any of them could've jimmied the locks and found what they wanted."

Brody gone. Lexie slowly breathed out, "J.J.?"

Tye squinted, "I can't get my head around J.J. as a killer. Brody was right about one thing—the workers. They did have access."

"We'll get on that tomorrow. I'll have the contractor list the men. Then I'll check for seedy histories and connections with any of the victims. Finally, a starting place in this investigation."

"Go on home, Sis. I'll mind the phone until J.J. finishes his rounds."

Lexie's instructions flowed, "Tell him we suspect a worker. Get his take on the situation. Ask why that folder was in his drawer. Also, wrap up Walkin's folder. We'll get it tested for prints and DNA in Tulsa."

"I'll do it."

"Tye pulled on plastic gloves and turned the pages of the Walkin report. Ten minutes into his research J.J. showed.

"What's up, Boss? Where's Brody?"

"He's pissed—walked out."

J.J. rubbed his baldhead. "Will I have reason to do the same?"

"We found Walkin's folder in your desk. Do you have any idea how it got there?"

"I haven't had a chance to look at the old case. Anyway, I always put the folders in Delia's re-file box. She gets riled if anyone messes up her system."

"That's for sure. I've gotten a tongue lashing twice for my sloppy ways. Was Brody here Friday night?"

"Nah, Myrna drug him to a church event. I stayed in the office after one trip around town."

"Did anyone drop by the office during the night?"

"No. I saw a few folks at Dixie's when I bought supper."

Redness seeped into J.J.'s complexion. "Am I a suspect in Walkin's murder?"

"You, Brody, and every man who worked here during the renovation."

"Can't blame Brody for his anger. I'm feeling shit-on myself."

"Lexie's new theory is that all the recent murders in our county, one a county over, and one investigated by Cherokee Nation are the result of a serial killer. Someone paying back people for harm they've done to others."

"I thought the Sheriff said Slick was behind the deaths."

"She changed her mind."

"Do you think I'm a killer?"

"Of course not, but you know how this works. We're ruled by procedures, not our guts."

"That makes me feel a little better."

Tye stood and stretched. "I'm driving to Tulsa to have this folder examined by the lab. No way I can sleep tonight. I'll see you tomorrow."

J.J. grimaced.

Tye almost apologized, but decided a declaration of J.J.'s innocence was premature.

CHAPTER TWENTY-THREE

The ice in the morning air sent a chill through Lexie. The Christmas decorations didn't lift her spirits. Missing the murder pattern weighed heavy on her conscience. She had Christmas morning surprises from Santa for Sky, but that ended her Christmas spirit. Early for work, she crossed the street to Dixie's for breakfast.

Two gold angel barrettes decorated Dixie's seasonal red hair. "You're an early bird."

"Not sleeping well with all the murder cases to solve."

"You'd better get it done, girl. Customers rumbling that you shouldn't have been re-elected. Folks are afraid to leave their houses. Ain't good for my business."

"I got rumblings, too," a voice called from a corner booth. "In my stomach, and your waitress disappeared."

"She's in the back. I'll get her."

" Lexie, I can't stay long, but come join me."

Her pulse quickened as she slid into the booth opposite her favorite Cherokee Marshal.

Gus started the conversation. "Sorry, I didn't answer your message yesterday. I planned to drop by your office after breakfast. What's up?"

"I think Leroy's killing is one of a series."

"Tell me more."

"The cases I'm investigating, yours, and a vehicular homicide out of county all have a common thread." Lexie took a drink of water.

"What's the connection?"

"The similarity, to state it biblically, is an eye for an eye. A child abuser beat to death, a porn guy with his penis cut off, and a drunk driver killed with a liquor bottle."

"And an Indian suspected of killing Hawk with an arrow shot to the heart is now dead from the same cause."

Gina shuffled to the table. "Marshal Farmer, I hear you're in a hurry for breakfast."

"Big breakfast plate to go. Coffee now."

"What's your poison, Sheriff Wolfe?" Gina wisecracked.

"Your attitude."

"Funny girl," Gina smirked.

"Bacon and egg biscuit to go and coffee for here."

"I'm happy to see your claws in a man other than my husband."

Gina's butt swayed as she sauntered to the next table.

Gus leaned in, "Red married one hateful woman. I should mail him a sympathy card."

"Sorry about that. She's under the delusion that I'm trying to take Red."

"Are you over him?"

"He left me. My only option was to move on."

Gus' broad shoulders slumped. "That doesn't give me confidence that you'd give another man a fair shake."

Lexie touched a sunbeam reflected on the tabletop. "Depends on the man."

"Is there any evidence to support your theory?"

"Well, Marshal, I've a folder that the killer probably touched. I hope he drank from the liquor bottle prior to smashing it into Walkin's head."

Gina brushed Lexie's arm as she set coffee on the table. She gently placed Gus' cup in front of him.

Lexie continued without looking up. "This morning, I'll get

names of workers who were in my office during the renovation. Someone had inside information in order to replicate Lindy's injuries. Anyone with night access to my records could've grabbed individual records, especially if they were looking for certain cases."

"You solve my case with yours, and I'll owe you a fancy city dinner."

"I'd happily collect."

"I'll review the Hawk case this morning and determine if there's a way I can tie in with your investigation."

"I'd appreciate it." She followed Gus to the cash register.

Gina handed him a to go box and Lexie a bag. "Have a good day, Gus," she said sweetly. Then snarled, "Good riddance" in Lexie's direction.

Lexie felt a peck on her cheek, "See you later, Honey."

"Can't wait!" Lexie responded with a smile.

The coins in Gina's hand rattled to the floor.

I'd like to kiss him square on the mouth. It takes an insightful man to crush Gina's attitude. Maybe if she thinks I've moved on, she'll lay off Sky and me.

Outside the restaurant door, Lexie patted his back, "Thanks."

"My pleasure," he answered.

Lexie ate her biscuit as she walked toward Clayton's office. His secretary's subdued greeting was likely the result of her boss's hatred for Lexie.

"I want ten minutes with Clayton. It's important."

"He's with someone."

Lexie lowered herself onto the sofa, "I'll wait."

Fifteen minutes later Clayton opened the door to let Slick out.

Slick eyeballed her, "Ah Sheriff are you resigning? Ready for a man to take over?"

"Lucky for the county I've decided to stay. It's hard to find a honest man these days."

"What do you want, Wolfe?" Clayton sniped.

Lexie sharpened her tone, "You have information related to the murder cases."

"Now you're tangling me in your accusations?"

"Good news men. It's beginning to look like Slick is innocent. You may help prove it, Clayton."

"Come in. Sit down. See you later, Slick."

Lexie, as always, was amazed at the richness of Clayton's office. The glass on the desktop covered an intricate wood carving of horses. Red and black plaid drapes matched two easy chairs and the throw cushions on a black sofa.

His eyes shot darts, "What do you want?"

"I've come to the conclusion that the murders were committed by the same person—a serial killer, who is playing God. Whoever committed these crimes had access to the confidential records in my office. Which means that all the workers who were in my office during the renovation are persons of interest."

"That's a dozen or more men."

"Give me the name and phone number of your contractor. Also, a list of anyone who worked on the project."

Clayton pulled a pen from the bronze box on his desk, then copied a number from his rotary directory. "His name is Daks McGee. I'll phone and tell him to get the list done then FAX it to you. What's your time line?"

"Tye took evidence to the Tulsa lab. It'll be two or three days before we get DNA results. I won't interview any of the workers prior to then. I'll need to crosscheck the killer with their DNA. The sooner I get the list the better. I'll check the names for criminal records."

"I'll tell McGee to deliver the list today."

"Please don't divulge why I want the names. The killer may get scared and take off."

"I'll tell Daks you're sending thank you notes to the workmen."

"Clever idea. Thanks for your help."

Lexie walked back into the cold crisp air. She was appreciative that Clayton was cooperative.

Maybe Slick did kill Bo, Rocky and Wilbur. Perhaps one or

more people committed the other murders. Disastrous when I don't know how many killers I need to find.

Tye greeted her with sleep deprived eyes and a shallow, "Hey, Sis."

"Can you stay awake while we talk?"

"You don't look too invigorated yourself."

"I was so obsessed with Clayton and Slick, I missed the pattern in these cases."

"Don't feel bad. I missed it, too, and I'm smart."

The corners of Lexie's mouth turned up, "Gee, good point."

"Perhaps multiple killers and Slick is one of them," Tye speculated.

"I thought of that."

"What's our next move?"

"Wait for the DNA results so we'll have something to match with the workers."

"Makes sense. Are you and Sky coming to the Christmas Eve service tonight?"

"Yes, she'll love the candles."

"You're invited to my house tomorrow."

"No, thanks. I'll take Sky to Red after she opens her Santa presents and eats breakfast. I'll hold down the fort tomorrow. Brody is covering for J.J. tonight."

"J.J. told me about visiting an aunt in Missouri for Christmas. First time he's mentioned a relative."

"Can you work all night on Christmas, Tye?"

"Sure. When will you question the workers?"

"The day after Christmas. Before then, I'll check for criminal records and connections with any of the victims."

"Sounds like a good plan."

"All I got for now, but in a week or less I hope this is over. I'm tired of the nasty newspaper articles and the mayor's vengeance."

CHAPTER TWENTY-FOUR

Sitting at her desk was an exercise in boredom after a fun Christmas morning with Sky.

The cold weather and Christmas festivities shut down Diffee. Even Dixie's restaurant was dark. The one-day a year she closed.

Lexie caught up on the avalanche of paperwork. Then she wandered the office thinking that 5 p.m. and Tye would never show up.

Her eyes scanned the fronts of the file cabinets, then her gaze backtracked to a drawer slightly ajar. Her hand gripped the pull and slid the drawer out slowly. One folder stuck up half-an-inch. Her fingers gripped the folder edge before it sank back into order. Walking toward her desk she read aloud. Her words didn't halt at Tye's entrance and friendly "Merry Christmas."

"Bob Daily was acquitted of the death of his estranged wife, Florence Daily. Florence died as a result of a knife wound to the neck. Jury found him innocent due to a lack of evidence. A witness, Hana Monroe, claimed Daily slept with her the night of the murder."

"What are you reading, Lexie?"

"Someone didn't straighten this folder back in the file."

"You think?"

"I think Mr. Daily is our next victim."

Lexie retrieved the phone directory from Delia's drawer. "He's listed."

The numbers pressed, a voice soon answered, "Bob Daily, here."

"Mr. Daily this is Sheriff Wolfe. Lock up your house."

"What's going on?"

"I think your life is in danger. I'll explain when I get there."

"Okay," he croaked.

"Lock-up. Right now."

"I will," he stammered.

Lexie tossed the keys to Tye. "Drop me off a couple blocks from the house. We can't have a patrol car near the place."

"With any luck," Tye added, "the killer will show tonight. Christmas isn't a day one expects a murderer to visit."

"True, even criminals have family functions to attend."

"After I leave you, I'll park our vehicle and jog to Daily's place."

···•••●●●•••···

"What's all the fuss about, Sheriff?" Daily's irritation simmered.

He and the witness, who'd covered his ass and saved him from prison, were apparently about to enjoy a candlelight dinner.

"I believe someone plans to kill you for murdering your wife."

"I was exonerated. I'm mighty damn tired of criminal treatment."

"At this juncture it doesn't matter whether you killed Florence or not. The killer makes his own justice."

The woman whined, "Will he kill me, too?"

"He cut out a liar's tongue. You can figure out if that has any relevance to you personally."

"How will you protect us, Sheriff?"

"Lock yourselves in the bedroom. Make sure the curtains are drawn and check the window latches."

"I'm afraid," Hana whimpered

Bob squeezed her hand, "I won't let anything happen to you, sweetheart."

Lexie continued, "Turn off all lights on the first floor, but leave the candles lit. Find me a dressy blouse. I want to look like Hana sitting at the table. My dark hair is a problem."

"I can help with that," Hana offered.

The women jogged up the steps. Hana pinned Lexie's hair up and placed a blonde wig. A red lace blouse finished the disguise.

When Tye arrived, he was handed Bob's dinner jacket. The seams stretched as Tye struggled his arms into the sleeves. Lexie tucked his hair under the jacket collar.

The Daily's were safely sequestered upstairs. Lexie and Tye sat opposite each other. Flickers of light showed apprehension on their faces.

Lexie smoothed her hand across the gold tablecloth. "Since it's so dark, I hope the killer will think we're his victims."

"There's a chance he doesn't know what Bob and the new Mrs. Daily look like. I'll unlock the back door for easy access. I don't want the killer to change his mind."

Lexie cradled a gun in her lap. The pair waited patiently the first hour. The second hour they discussed giving up, but didn't move from their chairs.

Two hours and one candle into the charade, a creaking door tightened Lexie's gut.

The door opened a foot and Hana whispered, "Lexie?"

The candle wavered as Lexie hit the table on her way to standing. She hissed, "What do you want, Hana?"

"It's past time for Bob's heart medicine. It's in the den."

"I'll get it. Where's it located?"

"Side table. I think."

"I'll find it. Get out of here."

Lexie opened the door. The medicine wasn't on or in the side table. Her eyes scanned every surface. No luck. She moved magazines aside to see if the pills were buried under clutter. Finally, the bottle fell to the floor when she shook a newspaper.

She took the stairs two steps at a time.

A deep, haunting voice spoke from behind Tye. An arm wrapped around his neck. "I'm the deliverer of righteousness. God called me to avenge the murder of your wife. My mission on earth is to strike down evil people. Today you must go to hell for your sins."

The glow of the candle picked up a gleam from the knife blade, right before a puff of the killer's breath extinguished the low flame.

He pulled up Tye's chin from behind and leveled the knife. A superficial cut circled the neck front from ear to ear. "This is how your wife felt. Feel her fear." He rubbed blood from the cut across Tye's lips, "Taste her fear."

Tye rocked with all his might.

The killer fell backwards. Tye and the chair smashed on top of him. Tye struggled to his feet. The man flung the chair, then grabbed Tye's ankle and pulled him to the floor. The man sat on his lower back and finished the knife circle around his neck. A stream of blood curved around his throat from the knife's point.

Lexie opened the door cautiously. For all she knew the killer was hidden in the kitchen ready to attack. Her heartbeat escalated as she saw the shapes of two men in the darkness.

The man spoke but didn't turn toward her. "Your only chance of survival is to go upstairs and let me escape. Go now, or I'll cut out your tongue. Then I'll kill you."

Lexie leveled her gun, "Drop the knife or you're dead."

"NO, LEXIE!" Tye yelled, then his words became strangely calm. "He's my son, the murderer."

The bloody knife slipped from Brody's hand as he struggled to his feet. Irrational babble flowed. "How dare you interrupt God's work? They all deserved to die. The legal system let them go free. I made them pay. I do God's work."

Tye secured the knife with his foot. "You're a murderer, Brody. No better than any of those evil people. Chances are you killed innocent men during your savagery."

Anger seeped into Brody's words, "You assumed Trey Moore's innocence because he tried to buy a place in heaven by helping kids."

Lexie's breath caught, She didn't consider that Trey's death was one in the series. "How about his wife? She's locked up for murder."

"She shouldn't have stayed married to the scum who killed her son."

Lexie phoned OSBI and J.J., then pushed Daily's phone number from her recently called list. "Hana, we're finished. The killer was apprehended. Bring down an old towel."

The handcuffs clicked around her nephew's wrists.

Hana ran into the room, "Is this okay?"

"Yes, Tye's throat needs wrapped."

Hana gasped, "Oh my God!"

"Wound isn't deep," Tye assured her. "Toss the towel."

Hana turned to Brody, "You crazy fool."

"Daily's evil and you'll rot in hell with him," Brody preached.

"Where's Bob?" Lexie asked.

"Still not feeling well. I'll tell him what happened."

"You two stay out of the dining room and kitchen until after the investigation. OSBI officers will arrive soon."

"I'll wait for them in the living room."

Lexie's spirit deflated as she held the gun at Brody's back. Tye kept a hand lock on the prisoner's arm so he wouldn't run. The three walked to the cruiser.

Back at the office, Tye shoved Brody into a cell.

"You never loved me. Never wanted me. I'm here because you and my so-called mother ruined my life. Both of you should fry in the electric chair with me—a family together forever in hell," Brody ranted.

Lexie fired back, "You made the choice to turn into a monster. Other people have traumatic childhoods and don't become murderers."

"I'm righteous. I get rid of evil people. I'm a better sheriff than you've ever been."

Tye's forehead touched the surface of his desk. Moisture escaped from his eyes.

Lexie spoke, but she feared Tye wasn't capable of listening. "J.J.'s back from Missouri. He'll finish the shift. I'll take you to the emergency room to have your neck checked. It's still bleeding. Houser will meet us there."

Lexie went in the restroom. She splashed water on her face. The events of the day ripped at her emotions. She knew her brother's pain was much worse.

CHAPTER TWENTY-FIVE

By 5 p.m., the day after Christmas, the Oklahoma State Bureau of Investigation confirmed that Brody drank from the same bottle that ended up lodged in Walkin's head.

Lexie looked up from the OSBI message. "What are you doing here? I told you to stay home."

"I can't listen to Jamie wail anymore. She blames herself for Brody's insanity. She screams for me to save him and no one can. Anyway, Jamie, Seth and Adam are coming to tell Brody goodbye. I want to be here with them."

Lexie stood, "J.J.'s out front. I'm going home."

Tye eyed Brody through the bars. His calloused exterior had softened since last night. The cockiness disintegrated into apprehension and fear.

He was thankful Brody confessed. A trial would've sucked the life out of Jamie and the rest of the family. Brody thought the truth would get him a life sentence instead of a lethal injection. Tye doubted that result considering Brody's history.

Jamie and Seth walked in silently, as if in a funeral progression.

"Where's Adam?"

"Told me he couldn't face Brody after all the people he killed." Jamie's face peered between the cell bars. "I'll never forgive myself for putting you up for adoption."

Brody's eyes filled with tears. "You didn't know the outcome. Don't blame yourself."

Jamie reached a hand between the bars and pulled him toward her. On tiptoes she kissed his forehead.

Seth positioned his arm between the bars. Brody's hand grasp the top of his arm then slid down to meet his fist bump.

Seth's face pinched as he tugged at the cell door. "Get Adam out of jail, Daddy."

The prisoner's face paled.

"Jamie, take Seth home. This is too much for him."

Seth pounded on the bars, "No, Daddy, no!"

Tye knelt and whispered in Seth's ear. "I promise Adam is okay. Go with your mom."

The pair gone, he phoned Dixie's restaurant. "It's Tye. Two steak dinners with baked potatoes and green beans to go."

"Last meal with your son?"

"Yep. I'll pick up in a few minutes."

Tye rolled his desk chair beside the cell. "Adam, you almost carried off the switch. If it wasn't for that special handshake with Seth, you'd have ruined the rest of your life."

Adam's shoulders bent forward as he paced. "The man who raped Brody messed up his brain and destroyed his life. He deserved another chance—an opportunity only I could give him."

Tye's jaw clenched, "Another chance to murder people?"

"Brody promised he wouldn't."

"Your brother is sick in the head—no control over his vengeance."

"He deserved a new life."

"You planned to go to prison, or death row in his place? Your brother would've been free to kill for the rest of his life. Was this his idea or yours?"

"I guess his, but I agreed. That way he can leave the country. In two weeks I'll admit we switched places."

"Did he mention that you'd serve jail time for aiding and

abetting a confessed serial killer? That you'd be locked up with the scum of society?"

"Brody said I'd have a real life story to write. One that will make me famous."

"Famous in prison doesn't sound glamorous. How did you switch places?"

"It was easy. Brody knew where the keys were stored. When J.J. went on rounds I unlocked the cell. We switched clothes and places."

Tye walked out the door.

Adam sank onto the bunk and chewed his nails.

A few minutes later, Tye returned with steak dinners. He unlocked the cell and motioned Adam to the conference table.

The occasional rattle of utensils was the only sound that interrupted the silence.

Halfway into the meal, Tye spoke. "Here's what will happen. "You'll beat me."

"No, Dad. I can't."

"You can and you will. Brody will escape tonight. Tomorrow you'll be yourself."

"Just let me go," Adam begged.

"I can't open a cell door and let a criminal out. I'd have charges filed against me or J.J. blamed."

"They'll hunt Brody down."

"He's a murderer. Everyone he kills between now and his capture is on your head."

"I can't hurt you, Dad."

"It's our only chance to fix this mess."

Tye startled as the back door opened.

J.J. rustled in, "What the hell are you doing? I got to lock him up."

"You don't look like you're feeling well. I'll work the night shift for you."

J.J. pulled out his gun and aimed it toward Adam. "Don't let him go. Brody's not worth ruining your life."

"But Adam is."

J.J.'s gun slipped back into its holster. "Adam?"

"Yes, they switched places. Tonight he'll escape to his old life. He won't beat me. They switched on your shift, your negligence. I'm thinking you'll make this right. Adam can walk out of here, and the cops may catch Brody before he kills someone else."

Without a word, J.J.'s iron fist pounded Tye's face. Blood squirted into the air.

"No!" Adam yelled.

"Shut up, before someone hears you. Get out of here. He threw Adam his truck key. Go to your apartment and resume your life. None of this ever happened."

"But Dad."

"GET OUT."

Adam ran into the cold night.

"I'll tell Lexie you were sick and I ordered you home. Now take this fork and jam it between my ribs," Tye pointed to the spot.

J.J.'s hand quivered as he followed the order.

The pain bent Tye, but he struggled into the jail cell without assistance. He didn't risk J.J. getting blood on his clothes.

"Beat me until I pass out. Be an Army vet, not a scared recruit."

J.J. attacked Tye's upper body with both fists.

Ten minutes later Tye mumbled, "Thank you, my friend. Finish me off and lock the cell door."

CHAPTER TWENTY-SIX

Lexie pulled into the front office space. A text from Tye the night before indicated J.J. went home sick. Tye worked a double shift with his deranged son present.

At the first glimpse inside, her heartbeat escalated. Broken glass, steak bones, pieces of potato, and knocked over chairs surrounded the conference table.

Her gaze fell on the battered body in the cell. "Tye," she yelped.

His eyes slowly pinpointed the sister who crouched over him. "Brody escaped."

"I'm calling an ambulance."

"He beat me, but I'm okay," Tye muttered.

She choked out words, "Doesn't look like you fought back."

"He's my son."

"The killer."

"Still my son. What are you doing?"

"Calling an ambulance, remember? There's a fork stuck in your ribs."

"You know that's a good point. I feel groggy."

"You're not making much sense."

"Hmm," Tye uttered.

"Send an ambulance to the sheriff's office. Physical attack on my deputy—a fork stuck in his rib cage."

Next she pushed in Houser's number. "Get men here ASAP. A prisoner escaped and Tye was beaten."

"We're on our way."

Minutes later, attendants lifted Tye into the ambulance.

"Take out the fork," he begged.

"Only a physician can remove the fork. We can't control bleeding in the ambulance."

As the siren squealed toward the hospital, Lexie phoned Jamie then Margo.

Delia arrived as Lexie hung up the phone.

Concern strained her speech. "What happened here?"

"Brody attacked Tye and escaped."

"OH NO. Is Tye okay?"

"An ambulance transported him to the hospital. Talked, but it was a bit goofy. I think he'll recover after the doctor removes the fork from his ribs."

Delia gasp, "Fork?"

"Looked like it hit between vital organs."

Delia shuffled toward the broom closet. "I better clean up this mess."

"We can't. They'll investigate first. My murdering nephew escaped on his father's watch which will probably end my job."

"That sounds bad, Lexie."

"Don't I know."

A vigorous knock sounded. Lexie rolled open the lock.

"Why you locked up?" Houser boomed. "Better not tamper with evidence."

"I thought it best to keep the public out. By the way, I didn't miss your accusation."

"What's the story?"

"Verify with Tye, but from what I learned he ate a last meal with his son. Brody beat him and locked him in the cell."

House's nostril's flared, "Shall I pretend that your brother couldn't take the kid?"

"I'm thinking he didn't try."

"Best you and Delia get out so we can investigate. Where was J.J. during all this?"

"He went home sick last night."

"Neither of us believe that, Sheriff. What's the truth?"

"He probably sent J.J. home. That way, Tye could spend last evening with Brody."

"I already put an alert out for your nephew. Every law enforcement agent in Oklahoma and the surrounding states are looking for him. I phoned the FBI. Your nephew has killed enough people to put the entire United States on lock down."

"Here's another one for you—he killed Trey Moore."

"That's a zinger. I have an innocent woman in solitary confinement in a mental health facility for that death. You and your family are pains in my ass."

"Give it a rest, Houser. Half your cases are now solved. You should thank me."

"If it wasn't for your homicidal nephew they wouldn't have existed. I lost sleep."

"Explains why you're so grouchy."

"Fact is, I'm always in a bad mood."

"May I tell Doris Moore? It'll save you a trip and give me the chance to apologize."

"That works. I'll call the hospital and get it cleared."

"After my confession to Doris, I'll check on Tye."

"I'll probably see you there, but first I'll investigate the crime scene."

"Remember he's innocent until proven guilty."

Sarcasm dripped from Houser's word, "Right."

·····●●●●●·····

The guard unlocked the door. Doris fisted and pulled the collar of her gown. A young woman sat in a straight back chair near the window.

"I'm Sheriff Lexie Wolfe from Diffee."

"I'm Doris' daughter, Amber."

Lexie stood in front of Doris. She placed her hands on either side of Doris' face. "You didn't shoot your husband. We have proof. A serial killer murdered him."

Amber sprang from her chair. "Mama, you're innocent. You did nothing wrong. I'm sorry I blamed you. I was cruel. Please forgive me."

Doris patted her head, "It's okay. I thought I killed him."

"Can I take her home, Sheriff?"

"Talk to her psychiatrist. They'll no longer treat her like a prisoner if she stays inpatient."

"Are you ready to go home, Mama?"

"I'll stay here a while longer—tired and sad. You say I didn't kill Trey?"

"No, Doris, you were so traumatized by his death you took on the guilt."

"After he shot Alan I wished him dead. I thought I finally killed him."

"Doris, you didn't kill your husband. You're innocent. I'm sorry for all the pain this has caused. The man who killed Trey was my nephew."

Doris placed a hand on Lexie's moist cheek. "It's not your fault, child."

CHAPTER TWENTY-SEVEN

Lexie sat in the background as Houser grilled Tye. After a series of questions asking for descriptions of events, Houser asked the important one: "Did you help Brody escape?"

"I didn't assist a homicidal maniac."

Lexie heard the certainty in his tone. For the first time, she thought there was a chance Tye didn't let Brody escape.

"You willing to take a lie detector test, Wolfe?"

"Yes."

"Get out, Lexie," Houser barked.

She moved to the lobby where Seth waited with Jamie.

"Lexie, will you stay with Seth while I take a restroom break?"

"Sure."

The sound of a whirling blade brought Seth to standing. She stood beside him and grasped his hand.

"Where's the helicopter going?"

"Probably taking someone who was hurt real bad to a bigger hospital."

"Daddy?" he gulped.

"No, you're daddy is recovering. He'll stay here."

"Hey," Adam called as he stepped off the elevator.

Seth's voice sang across the hall. "I knew Daddy would get

you out of jail."

Lexie felt her insides turn to mush as she witnessed Adam's anxiety. *Oh my God!*

CHAPTER TWENTY-EIGHT

On the third day after his beating, Lexie watched her bruised and bandaged brother limp to his desk.

"No luck finding Brody," she announced.

"I'm sure he's long gone."

"Plenty of time to get away," Lexie stated.

Tye squinted, "You think I purposely let him loose?"

"I don't think you'd let a serial killer escape."

"That's good to know."

A blast of sound brought Lexie to her feet. Her eyes wild. Her hand struggled to release the gun from her holster.

Tye held his crutch like a weapon, "What the hell?"

Two officers crashed through the back door and two through the front. Weapons drawn and faces angry.

"Put down the gun, Sheriff."

The sounds of Clayton and Slick's entries echoed in the aftermath of Houser's order.

Clayton's venomous tongue spouted, "It's time for your exit. You not only lost this fight, you lost the war."

Lexie's eyes searched Houser's face, "What's this about?"

"You're removed from office pending an investigation of your nephew's escape."

"Most of the folks in Diffee think you two conspired to set a murderer free, and now you'll pay."

"Let up, Slick," Houser ordered. "Sheriff Wolfe, you're removed, with pay, until my investigation ends. The mayor has selected Slick to serve in the interim. If you have any personal belongings here, get them. I'll escort you and Tye out in exactly five minutes."

Lexie collected a bag of personal items then handed her badge and gun to Houser. Tye did the same.

"Goodbye and good riddance, Wolfe siblings," Clayton hollered at their exiting backs.

The two stood on the front sidewalk. "That smile on Clayton's face was as rare as an eagle sighting," Lexie commented.

"I'm sorry, Sis. My family screwed up your life."

"Your family is my family. We'll get paid until the investigation comes to an end. I'll worry about a new job, in a different place, after that happens."

"Stay with us."

"If the worse happens, Sky and I'll stay with Mom until I find a new job."

"In the meantime?"

Lexie forced a laugh, "I'm taking a vacation. Isn't that what all unemployed people do?"

"You're still going on Sloan and Delia's wedding cruise?"

"Nothing better to do, and they've already paid for our tickets."

"You're right. We might as well take a trip before joining the unemployment line."

"My thought exactly."

"Get in my truck, Sis. I'll drop you off at home since they confiscated your patrol car."

"No thanks. A walk will clear my head." Lexie turned toward home.

She heard Tye's words at her back, "I'm sorry."

"I know," she called back without turning her tear stained face.

CHAPTER TWENTY-NINE

Chill bumps popped up on Adam's arms and a pain settled in his belly. He blurted into the phone, "Who's this?"

"Who the hell do you think?" Remember me—the brother you betrayed. I'm on the fire escape. Open the back window before someone sees me."

"You're here?"

"Hurry, fool."

Brody bent his body and squeezed through the small window. He straightened, then sent a piercing stare through his brother.

"I didn't do it on purpose. Seth recognized me. I started our special handshake without thinking and he knew it was me."

"You damn fool. Now I can't drive into Mexico because they'll check my ID at the border. My photo is probably posted in every convenience store between here and Mexico."

Adam's voice was barely audible, "You should turn yourself in."

"You're crazy man. My future doesn't include a jail, a trial, and a lethal injection."

Adam's words rattled out, "What do you expect after all the people you killed?"

"I don't appreciate your smartass mouth, particularly since you put me in this situation."

"Your criminal activity has nothing to do with me."

"I keep forgetting that you're the blessed, golden twin. I'm the bad one who's persecuted for killing evil people. Each and every one of them deserved to die. I did God's work."

"God doesn't want a judge and axman."

"Don't you dare belittle my good work."

"Why are you here, Brody?"

"I'm taking Delia and Sloan's wedding cruise in your place. I'll get off at the first port and never return."

"I won't help you."

"You owe me."

"I've never seen Dad so bad. I can't hurt him again. He had J.J. beat him, and claimed you did it so I wasn't an accessory to your escape."

"Daddy Tye saved your ass and left mine in a grinder—typical."

"Me in jail. Does that even faze you?"

"You'd get out soon enough and your brother free instead of rotting in prison. Let's discuss my cruise plans."

"I said NO. I won't help you. Lexie and Dad were both removed from their jobs pending an investigation into your escape. Judge Simpson won't let Gabriel go home because of Dad's involvement in all your crap."

"My life is more important than their jobs or that whiny little boy."

"Not to me—you're a freaking psychopath and I'm not giving into your insanity again."

"Listen up, asshole. You'll do as I say, or your dear daddy and mommy will die. Remember, I kill evil people."

"They aren't evil."

"They gave me to a child rapist."

"You know there's more to the story. They never intended for that to happen."

"Says the brother who ended up with the good life. What's my schedule tomorrow?"

"I'll ride with Dad, Lexie, Sloan and Delia to the airport. We fly to Fort Lauderdale, then get on the ship."

"Jamie isn't going?"

"She didn't want to miss work, or take Seth out of school."

"Are they picking you up?"

"Yes, at 6 a.m. I don't think you can fool them."

"I'm not a screw up like you. I'll do great as my wimpy brother. I'll pretend I'm half a man. Anyway, I'll sleep my way to the ship. Do you have a cabin by yourself?"

"Originally, it was for both of us. Where do you plan to get off?"

"Belize is a nice sunny place to live. Is my bag packed?"

"Mine is packed."

"It's my bag now. I'll sleep in the bedroom tonight. You sleep on the sofa."

"Aren't you afraid the airport authorities will recognize you?"

"I have your identification. With luck I'll get past them. Not to mention the advantage of having a sheriff and deputy with me. They'll trust a pair of their own."

Adam shook his head, "That's a big risk."

"It's my only chance. Come to think of it, maybe not. I can always tell them where Brody is hiding in Diffee. They'll knock down your door and take you to jail."

"You're a demon."

Brody's hand grasped Adam's chin. "If you screw up I'll be a demon on your daddy. Tell me all the plans for this trip. If they told you, then I hear it."

In a dull tone, Adam gave his brother trip information.

"That all?" Brody asked.

"Oh, I forgot one thing. I'll stick Delia's card in your suitcase. I told her I'd have a wedding day surprise for them."

"Tell me what I bought."

"I wrote a newspaper article about them. Interviewed a dozen people who talked about the positive influences one or both of them were in their lives. Boss gave me an early edition. I'll cut the article and put it in a manila envelope with their card."

Brody's face squeezed as if a bad odor crossed his nose, "Such a sweet boy."

"Smile and act sneaky when you hand it to Delia. I've teased her for days about my secret present. If you act nonchalant, it'll be a dead giveaway that something is wrong."

"I can handle it. I'm not clueless like my brother."

Adam slowly cut out the article and attached photo.

"Man, you aren't giving the stupid thing to the queen."

"It's a gift, I want it cut straight. Make yourself useful and get us beers. Better still, I'd like a rum and coke."

"You think I'm your bartender?"

"This is our last night together, forever. Let's forget the past and say goodbye in peace."

"I'm willing," Brody moved toward the kitchen.

Adam heard the fridge door open and ice tingling into a glass. He scrawled a note on the card, licked the envelope, and pressed it shut.

Brody handed him the rum.

The ice jiggled, but Brody was too busy gulping his beer to notice Adam's hand tremble, or the fear in his eyes.

CHAPTER THIRTY

Lexie rang Tye's doorbell with one hand and grasp her wandering toddler with the other.

Seth swung the door open, "I'll take Sky's bag

"Thanks. I chased Sky while maneuvering the bag."

Seth slid the bag from Lexie's shoulder. "I'll put it on Gabriel's bed."

Jamie picked up the toddler, "You look frazzled."

"I didn't pack until last night. I washed laundry at midnight. It's more restful to stay home than take a vacation."

Jamie agreed, "That's my experience. I'm sorry about the Brody drama."

Lexie looked at the floor, "It is what it is."

"We feel terrible your job is in jeopardy."

"I'll force myself to have a good time for Delia's sake. A grouch isn't appreciated at a wedding."

Tye tugged an overstuffed suitcase into the room. "Come sit on the bag, Seth. I can't get it closed."

"You're more a clothes horse than me, Bro."

"You don't pack suit jackets. They take up too much space. Women wear skimpy clothes."

Jamie joined in, "Remember you're a married man. When you get all prettied up the girls may flock after you."

"Only thing that'd flock after me are vultures wanting brown meat for dinner."

He clicked the suitcase shut thanks to Seth's butt pressure.

"You better get going," Jamie warned. "Delia will hyperventilate if you're late."

"We're out of here." He firmly kissed Jamie's lips, then messed Seth's hair followed by a smooch on the forehead.

Lexie scooped Sky from the floor. "Aunt Jamie will take care of you until your daddy picks you up after nap time. Love you a million." Lexie pecked half dozen kisses on the small face.

The tiny lips puckered and landed directly on Lexie's mouth. "Love, Mommy."

Emotion swelled in Lexie's chest. She moved out the door behind Tye, never glancing back.

"You okay?"

"Hard to leave my girl."

"We'll pick up Adam, then drive to Delia's place. Sloan's our chauffer."

"That works," Lexie responded.

Fake Adam jogged down the steps of his garage apartment after one honk.

"Your son is eager to leave town."

"No kidding: he's never moved that fast before."

The door slammed and the new passenger buckled his seat belt.

"Are you ready for a vacation, son?"

"A reporter wants adventure, not stuck in rural Oklahoma."

"You don't want to come home," Lexie assumed.

"Nah, I want a break, not a change in residence."

"As your father, that's good news."

Sloan and Delia stood on the front porch and watched Tye turn into the driveway.

"Better get a move on, Dad. Delia's got her evil eye pointed this way."

"That's for damn sure."

The threesome retrieved their bags and dropped them into Sloan's trunk.

Delia honked the horn as they crowded into the back seat. "Seat belts fastened? Let's go. I don't want to miss my own wedding."

Sloan heeded her urgency and peeled out like a teenager. "I'll get you to the church on time, woman."

"Husband-to-be, don't you mean ship?"

"First I have to get to the airport."

"Get a move on."

"Yes, wife-to-be."

CHAPTER THIRTY-ONE

"Why's this line moving so damn slow?"

Lexie turned to face the elderly woman who uttered the sharp words. "A photographer is taking photos of each family group as they get on the ship."

"Oh bull shit. I'm seventy-nine, too old to stand in line forever. My son is the captain of this ship and I'm herded in like the rest of the cows."

"You go in front of us," Delia offered.

"Carry my bag, boy."

"I'm a guest on the ship, not your servant."

"What's your name, Mr. Guest?"

"Adam Wolfe."

"The Biblical Adam," she hissed. "The one who ate of the forbidden apple and ruined life for the rest of us for eternity."

"It wasn't me personally," Brody snapped.

"Give it a rest, son." Tye reached for the woman's bag. "I'll carry that for you."

"An Injun with manners—glory be."

"I'm Cherokee."

"Whoopi, all the same to me."

Tye's reddening skin contrasted sharply with his white shirt.

The woman shook her head. "You white folks are akin to

these Indians?"

"Yes," Delia answered. "They accepted and loved me when my family died off."

"I guess it takes all kinds."

"Apparently so," Lexie muttered.

"You'd be pretty if it weren't for that ugly scar on your face. How'd you get it?"

"I was killing a big-mouthed, white man and he slashed my face."

The woman's right hand pressed her chest, "Oh my, did he die?"

Lexie winked, "Not that day, but eventually I killed him."

Delia intervened, "She's a sheriff."

"Had me going for a minute. Afraid I'd end up scalped."

"What's your name?" Sloan asked.

"Mabel Schwinn. You?"

"I'm Sloan and this is Delia. Tomorrow she'll be my wife."

"What time? I don't have plans. My son's been a captain for fifteen years and this is the first time he's invited me on his ship. He told me, at least ten times, I'd be on my own."

Tye handed her the suitcase. "The photographer motioned for you, Mrs. Schwinn. They'll keep you moving forward after the photo, so you better take your bag."

"Your help didn't last long."

"Don't want you to get separated from your luggage."

She drug the bag toward the photographer. He lost his smile after one remark from Mabel's red lips.

Sloan turned toward the next families. "You folks go ahead of us. That grabby old biddy invited herself to my wedding and I don't want to tell her, hell no." Three groups moved forward before Sloan eased his party back into the photographer's line.

Lexie managed a smile for the family photo, then followed them to the ship's entry. She scanned faces and planned to detour if Mabel's glum face materialized.

Settled in the buffet area with plates filled with food, the five glanced at people passing.

Brody forked his sliced beef. "That old woman is a joke with that fake tan and blonde hair."

"Try a little understanding. It isn't easy growing old," Delia empathized.

Brody's tone softened, "I thought little old ladies were sweet."

Sloan responded, "Depends on the life they lived. However, kindness aside, that hateful mouth isn't going to wreck our wedding."

Delia squeezed his arm, "Amen to that."

Tye finished his coffee. "Four thousand people on this ship. It's not likely we'll see her again. Hard to track us down without our last name."

Delia pointed at Brody, "Adam said his last name. However, she was so hung up on the biblical Adam she probably didn't pay attention."

"Okay, son, if that woman stalks us it's your fault."

"The sins of the son never end."

Delia smiled, "If Mabel finds us, it'll be your worse sin yet."

Sloan swallowed a last bite of pie. "Let's go unpack and meet at 5 o'clock for dinner. A nap is in my near future."

CHAPTER THIRTY-TWO

Lexie craved alone time. At home she was cheerful for Sky. Away from her daughter there was no motivation to pretend happiness.

She and Delia shared a room tonight. After the wedding, Lexie was free to wallow in self-pity. Tye had Adam to partner with on the excursions; she'd find a way to separate herself. The way her stomach felt an excuse was true.

"Your turn in the bathroom," Delia announced.

"That pink pant suit looks pretty."

"Thanks, honey. I bought a few new things for the trip."

"As well you should for your honeymoon."

"Get moving girl."

"I'm a little nauseated from the ship motion. I've had a weak stomach for as long as I can remember."

"There are free meds in the infirmary."

Lexie pulled on white slacks and a green top. She braided her hair and dusted on face powder. "I'm ready."

Delia knocked next door to get Tye, then two doors down for Adam. Sloan was two decks up in the honeymoon suite. He met them at the dining room entrance.

Five minutes after sitting a voice shrieked, "Wolfe."

"Oh no," Lexie fisted her napkin, "the matriarch of meanness has found us."

"Too bad Brody isn't in that extra chair," Delia lamented.

"Something else Brody ruined," Lexie chided.

"Don't talk about my brother."

Lexie didn't respond to her nephew's gruff words.

"Mrs. Schwinn requested the extra chair at your table. Is that okay?" The waiter asked.

"Yes," Delia answered before anyone protested.

Mabel handed her cane to Brody, then tugged her chair out. "I had trouble finding you folks. Glad I remembered your weird last name. When I arrived at my cabin, I realized I missed the wedding time."

"We paid for the smallest ceremony," Delia explained. "We can't invite extra guests or the charge increases."

"My son will fix that—he's the big shot on this ship. Tell me the time and he'll arrange everything."

"My future wife is too polite, Mrs. Schwinn. We only want family at our ceremony—no outsiders."

"Have it your way. The Captain's mother at a wedding is an honor. I planned to invite you to join me at the Captain's table tomorrow night. Since I'm an *outsider* you won't receive that invitation." Her chair hit the floor when she pushed it back. She bellowed, "I won't eat with these heathens."

A maître d' rushed to her aid. "Come, Madame, I'll find you a table with a view."

The waitress who offered the Wolfe party an assortment of rolls, cowered back as Tye pointed to his selection.

"We really aren't heathens," Delia assured her.

The young woman didn't return to the Wolfe table. Her wary glances scrutinized the heathens as she served nearby tables. Her replacement was tall, muscular and male.

"That old woman is evil."

Delia reprimanded, "Don't talk that way, Adam. Likely she turned bitter due to a difficult life."

"Like my brother?"

Sarcasm stilted Lexie's words. "Killer is a long way from bitter."

The waiter cleared his throat, "Dinner selections, please."

The conversation turned to wedding plans and delicious food.

Lexie squinted and flexed the left side of her upper lip when she caught anyone staring at the heathen table.

CHAPTER THIRTY-THREE

Lexie awoke to a stomach agitating like a washing machine. She switched out of pajamas and scrawled a note to Delia. *Going to infirmary for nausea medicine.* She considered cancelling breakfast and lunch, but 6 a.m. was too early to think about meals.

Rumblings from the ship invaded the quiet as she found her way to the lowest deck.

The sleepy environment from the upper decks turned to mayhem as the elevator door opened. Suspicious eyes followed her. Two men in uniform stood outside the infirmary door.

"What's going on?" Lexie asked.

A broad-faced man shouted, "Why are you here?"

"Nausea meds."

"There," he pointed. "Get it from that box hanging on the wall."

"What happened?"

"None of your concern. Get your pills and go."

"Where's your Chief Security Officer?"

"Guy quit couple hours before the ship left shore."

Lexie read his tag. "Sampson, I'm in law enforcement. Where's the Captain."

His head shook, "Not a good time."

"It's a perfect time—get him."

"He's with his mother."

"Mabel?"

"You know her?"

"She's a friend," Lexie lied. "Where is she?"

"Mabel's dead."

The sweat creeping from Lexie's armpits felt like slithering snakes. "What's the cause of death?"

One uniformed man looked at the other. "Someone strangled the old bat."

"Hush, Sampson," the second man berated. "Don't talk ill of the dead."

"You know Mabel?" Lexie stated.

He ran a hand over his tight curls. "Long enough for her to insult my heritage."

"Knowing Mabel that didn't take long."

"For sure," Sampson acknowledged.

Lexie walked between the pair. Neither man attempted to stop her.

She halted at the examining room entrance: unwrapped, popped and swallowed dry pills, then knocked on the metal door.

A voice boomed, "WHAT?"

"I'm Sheriff Lexie Wolfe from Oklahoma. I'm here to investigate Mabel's murder."

The Captain's words faltered, "By whose authority?"

"I have a professional obligation to make sure murderers don't go free."

"Okie sheriffs are country people, not qualified to handle murders at sea."

"It's okay, Doc. We don't have a Chief Security Officer. I think a girl sheriff investigating might keep the main office off our backs."

Lexie wondered about the calmness of the man who stood next to his murdered mother. "Why don't you have a chief?"

"Chief took ill right before we embarked. Didn't have time to replace him."

"Who's next in command?"

"That's Elijah Sampson," Captain paused. "The problem is — he's a suspect."

"Tye, my deputy, is on the ship. He can assist with the investigation."

Dr. Van rubbed his forehead. "Amateur hour: Captain, you shouldn't let these people get involved."

"They can't hurt anything. Too late for Mabel."

"Where was she killed?"

"In her cabin."

"I'll check it out. Cause of death?"

"Strangulation," Van answered.

Lexie lifted the sheet from Mabel's face. "Any other injuries, Doctor?"

"No," he scowled.

Lexie visually examined the finger imprints on the front of Mabel's neck. "She was strangled from behind. Probably didn't see the attacker. Take me to the murder site, Captain."

She followed Schwinn up the back stairs.

He stopped on the stairwell and faced her. "Keep this quiet, Sheriff. I don't want spooked cruisers."

"I understand your position, but if we can't find an answer quick they need warned. For all we know the killer may attack someone else."

"It's an isolated event."

"How do you know?"

"I run a tight ship. Many of my subordinates despise me. I think someone murdered my mother for revenge."

"A good theory, but no proof. We'll wait a few hours before alerting the passengers. No disembarkations until the killer is found."

"The passengers will raise hell, and file law suits."

"That's nothing compared to dying on vacation."

Captain climbed the steps without rebuttal. Lexie followed him into Mabel's cabin. The space was neat—nothing out of place.

No sign of a struggle. "Who found the body?"

"Maid came in last night to turn down the covers. She found Mabel face down on the mattress."

"Why was her body moved?"

He avoided eye contact, "I sought medical assistance—my first reaction."

"Was she alive?"

"No," Captain defended, "I was shocked, didn't act logically."

"Who do you think killed your mother?"

"She embarked yesterday. Didn't know anyone. I heard she called her dinner partners heathens."

"For your information, I'm one of the heathens."

"You flamed her fiery temper?"

"We told her only family members were invited to my friend's on-board wedding."

"Due to your argument with Mom, I have no doubt that diners will point a finger at you and yours."

"Likely, but the truth is your mother was angry, not vice versa. You mentioned earlier that someone on the crew might want revenge. Who are your enemies?"

"I've disciplined at least half the crew at one time or other. I have no tolerance for fools, especially on my ship."

"Make me a list. Give me an hour, then have one of your men send the haters to me at thirty-minute intervals. I'll take samples from this cabin, then check Mabel's body for more. I'll work on this until 3 p.m., and then I'll attend my friend's wedding. Was the FBI contacted?"

An abrupt, "No," shot from his mouth.

"Do that before the list."

"Curtail your orders, Sheriff. This is my ship."

"Your ego is irrelevant when there's a murderer aboard."

Captain snarled then exited.

Lexie collected samples in Mabel's room then stopped at the computer lab.

She sent a note to Stan, a detective friend, and asked him to get answers. The main question was why the Senior Security Officer quit right before departure.

As soon as she entered, Dr. Van left the examining room.

She noted the time and considered her self-imposed schedule. Four hours designated for sample gathering and questioning haters. The rest of the day belonged to Delia and Sloan.

After three hours, Schwinn's designated haters were interviewed. Sampson, who Schwinn considered a suspect, never showed.

It took an hour of wandering and questioning anyone, and everyone, in uniform before she ended up face-to-face with Sampson.

"Who made you the keeper of Mabel Schwinn?"

"Captain."

"Why is that?"

His jaw clenched, "So I'd get shafted if something went wrong."

"Did you like Mabel?"

"My assignment."

"Did Captain tell you anything about her?"

"Said she was a sweet old lady, and dear to him. I'd better make sure she was happy."

"How did she treat you?"

He stepped back, "Like shit."

"Racial slurs?"

"Yes, the old shrew demeaned the Afro-American race."

"I understand. She took a few jabs at Native-Americans as well. Did you strangle her?"

Sampson's lips parted, "No, did you?"

Lexie smiled. "Sewing her lips together was my first choice. Do you have any idea who killed her?"

"No. I escorted her to the stateroom after the musical—around 8:30 p.m. She demanded that I check for an intruder. I looked around then made sure the door locked behind me."

"Did you notice if the bed covers were turned down?"

"Yes. I remember because Mabel grabbed the towel bunny from her bed, slammed it on the floor and shouted, 'foolishness!'"

"That's all for now, Sampson. One more thing, who hates the Captain enough to kill his mother?"

"Only a coward kills a mother instead of the man he hates."

"That makes sense. Thanks for your time."

Lexie jogged to her cabin. A warm shower, then she filed and painted her nails. The royal blue dress she slipped over her head was the one she wore for her own rehearsal dinner. She didn't think it bad luck. That night was wonderful. The actual wedding day was the disaster.

CHAPTER THIRTY-FOUR

The joy on Delia's face was more a glow than a mere emotion.

Lexie straightened the short white veil then lowered the net over her face. "You look beautiful! That blue dress makes your eyes sparkle."

"I cleaned up pretty well for an old girl."

"You look gorgeous compared to any age girl. Are you ready for a short trip down the aisle to a wonderful future with Sloan?"

"I've never been more ready for anything."

Recorded organ music played as Lexie half-stepped toward the minister, Tye and Sloan. She winked at Adam, the lone observer, as she passed.

The rhythm of the music changed to the wedding march. Delia walked slowly forward, visually zeroing in on Sloan.

"Wow," Sloan whispered as she stopped at the altar. "I have good taste."

"Me too," she responded.

The minister's words flowed and ended with "Until death do you part, and you may kiss the bride."

Lexie felt hollow inside as she witnessed their love. A long time since anyone cared that much for her.

"Time for dinner," Delia announced after her return trip down the aisle.

At their reserved table, they passed champagne, made toasts, and ate dinner followed by wedding cake.

Adam raised a glass. "Congratulations to the newlyweds. I hope you like my wedding gift."

"Where is this mysterious gift?" Sloan asked.

"I slid it under your suite door."

"A skinny present," Delia jested.

"I'm excusing myself. I met a hot girl at the bar last night. If I'm lucky she'll show again tonight."

"You go, Adam," Sloan advised. "Good to find true love before you're seventy."

Tye used the tabletop to balance his upward movement. "I'm taking pain pills and laying low until the morning. Goodnight."

Lexie raised her glass for a final toast. "I love you two, and wish you many years of happiness."

Delia smiled, "We love you, too."

Sloan's glass hesitated at his lips. "I'll drink to that."

A triple hug outside the dining room entrance ended the wedding celebration.

····•••●●●•••····

Lexie passed bar areas, heard singing float from the auditorium, and watched couples pose in front of a giant ship photo as she wandered the ship. Pictures from the art gallery lined the walls. Maybe tomorrow she'd sip champagne during the art auction, and pretend there was more than three hundred dollars in the bank.

Her mind returned to the Captain's ultimatum not to tell the passengers about the murder. She disagreed loudly, but it was his ship, his decision. Schwinn thought the killer only wanted one death—the one that impacted the ship's captain.

Schwinn's dismissive attitude was familiar. She'd dealt with the same attitude most days since she became the first female sheriff in Diffee. There was one more day before the cruisers exited the ship for excursions. One day left to apprehend the killer before he debarked in Belize.

The computer lab beckoned her, but she doubted that Stan answered this soon. She clicked on a computer.

Stan's message was to the point. Schwinn fired his Chief Security Officer—a man with a near perfect employment record. Within the last year, the captain purchased a two million dollar life insurance policy on Mabel. FBI wasn't notified of a murder on the ship.

Lexie headed toward bed.

A glint of light seeped out as she pushed open the cabin door. "What are you doing here?"

Delia fluttered an envelope in the air.

"What's that?"

"My gift from Adam."

Lexie sat on the sofa beside her. "Couldn't it wait until tomorrow?"

"No. Adam sent an article about our wedding, with a special note."

"Okay."

"Read the back of the card," Delia directed.

Lexie shivered as the meaning of Adam's message became apparent. *Delia, warn Dad and Lexie that Brody took my place on the ship. He threatened to kill Dad and Mom if I didn't cooperate. He'll escape in Belize. I'm sorry, Adam.*

Lexie moved to the bed and sank into the mattress.

Delia's hands fluttered, "Do you think Brody killed Mabel?"

"It's likely."

Delia fiddled with her robe tie. "He called Mabel evil."

"I remember."

"He accused the people he murdered in Diffee of evil."

"A huge coincidence, perhaps?" Lexie shook her head, "but that's doubtful."

"What will you do?"

"I'll walk you back to your room, then wake up Tye."

"Will he let Brody escape—again?"

"I don't know, Delia, but I want his thoughts on this disaster."

After Delia was safely back with Sloan, Lexie knocked on Tye's door.

She jumped as a low voice propelled warm breath near her ear.

"Dad hurt and took pain pills, Aunt Lexie. Why are you bothering him?"

"Can't sleep: I felt like screaming over my lost job."

"Leave Dad alone, you can bitch in the morning."

"By then I may cool down," Lexie protested.

"Go to bed," Brody ordered. "You apparently can't hold your liquor."

"Who was that pretty girl I saw sneak into your room?"

"My private business."

"You sure are snarly, Adam."

"That's what happens when you attack my father."

"I drank a couple extra Amaretto sours."

"Or three or four extras?"

"Very funny, nephew. Sleep tight and I hope your little girlfriend doesn't bite."

"Look who's attempting humor."

"Goodnight. Thanks for saving Tye from his drunken sister."

"Anytime."

Lexie's body swayed as she returned to her cabin. She didn't risk trying to access Tye again. Sinister thoughts crawled in her brain. *Was I a convincing drunk? Does he know that I suspect he's not Adam?*

She propped a shoe in the door and sat on the floor—waiting and listening for Brody's door to open. *With the pretty girl in his room, perhaps he'll take a night off from killing.*

CHAPTER THIRTY-FIVE

The door pushed against Lexie's sleeping body.

"Why is your shoe stuck in the door, Sis? Better still why are you on the floor?"

She grabbed the handle and pulled to standing. "Come in."

"Those dark circles around your eyes put a raccoon to shame. Did you have a wild night?"

"Did you talk to your son this morning?"

"He checked on me. Adam mentioned you went over your liquor capacity. Also, said you were fighting mad about your lost job."

"Brody...."

"Don't worry about it," he interrupted. "You have every right to feel angry. Better to let it out. I'm feeling better today. Came by to see if I can assist with Mabel's case."

She handed him Adam's message.

Lines in his forehead deepened. "Damn Brody to hell." His hand grasped the door handle.

"NO." She pushed a hand against the door. "Don't go."

""I'll beat the crap out of him."

"You can hardly move, much less beat up a punk half your age. There's a decision to make. He may have murdered Mabel."

"That thought hadn't entered my mind—yet."

137

"According to Adam's note, Brody will escape at the first port of call. Do you want him to go free?"

"You're letting me decide?"

"I don't want this on me. Tell me what you think."

"Not a hard decision. We'll get him locked up, then transported off the ship."

"That's what I hoped you'd say."

Lexie rang the Captain's room. "Schwinn, send armed security. Got a man who needs locked in the brig."

"Did you catch Mabel's killer?"

"Not sure, but I know this guy is wanted for murder."

"We'll be right there."

The Captain soon arrived, backed by three broad-shouldered seamen. The men flattened against the wall beside Brody's door.

Tye knocked, "Open up, son."

The door opened, "You sick, Dad?"

"The Captain has something to say."

Schwinn's upper lip flexed, "As Captain of this ship I'm arresting you for the murder of Mabel Schwinn. You have the right to remain...."

"Hell no, you're not pinning that old lady on me. You got no proof and I have rights. My brother's the murderer, not me."

"You are your brother," Lexie stated.

Schwinn snickered, "He can't be his own brother."

Lexie explained, "Brody took his brother's place on this cruise to escape murder charges in Oklahoma."

"I'm Adam. Brody tricked you."

Tye's hand grasped the neck of Brody's t-shirt and ripped. A black-eyed snake tattoo peeked from between the fringed edges. "Unfortunate for you, that Adam decided on a blue-eyed snake."

"Handcuff and lock him up," Lexie ordered.

Two strong hands pulled Brody's arms back and clicked the rings around his wrists. Sampson held a gun twelve inches from his back as the security entourage proceeded toward the elevator.

Brody turned with a jerk. Sampson cocked his gun and aimed.

"When I escape, Aunt Lexie, I'll kill you first. By the way, I didn't murder Mabel and I didn't cut out Wilbur's tongue. About time you looked at another relative for Wilbur's murder. I was taking the blame for my father, but now I won't protect the bastard."

Sampson shoved Brody forward.

"Sheriff, come to my office," Schwinn demanded.

·····•••●●●••·····

He settled into his oversized chair. "Brody killed Mabel. There's no reason to keep cruisers on the ship tomorrow. They can disembark and have a good time."

"I can't sanction that action. I don't actually know who killed your mother. Have you heard from the FBI?"

"Whoa girl. You don't have jurisdiction on my ship. You're lucky I let you play cop. Now it's about angry customers, and financial loss when they demand their money back."

"Television news and the internet will report how you risked these people's lives for the cruise company's bottom line."

"A threat from the sheriff, who brought a serial killer on my ship? You have a fool's nerve. You know your nephew killed Mabel."

"You're a more likely candidate."

"Based on what?"

"There's that mega money life insurance policy you bought."

"Mabel insisted I buy it to protect my financial future."

"You assigned an Afro-American to oversee her voyage. You knew she'd never keep her bigoted mouth shut, which set Sampson up as a suspect."

"You have a devious imagination, Sheriff."

"Then there's the well-timed firing of a Senior Security Officer with a perfect employment record."

Schwinn's eyelids flickered rapidly.

"I forgot to mention that you didn't contact the FBI after her death. Also, you lied about the maid finding Mabel's body."

"GET OUT."

She saluted, "Yes, sir."

CHAPTER THIRTY-SIX

Lexie's heartbeat escalated and echoed through her body. The cabin door opened slowly. Her right hand slid across the nightstand, then back under the cover. She lay still, as the intruder approached.

"Aunt Lexie," boomed out in a spray of bad breath.

Her eyes opened. "I wasn't expecting your company tonight. How did you escape?"

"Some generous soul left my cage door unlocked. As if that wasn't kind enough, my benefactor also left a key to your room, and this handy knife." Brody waved a six-inch knife in front of her face.

"I bet it was someone who heard you say you'd kill me first."

"Lucky me—given the sweet opportunity to slice and dice dear Aunt Lexie."

She sat up. "The Captain or Sampson, I bet. He was the guard who held the gun at your back. One of them wanted rid of me and you played right into their hands. Didn't realize the degree of your gullibility—disappointing."

The blade glimmered in his hand. "I don't give a damn as to why a stranger assisted me."

"I think Captain killed Mabel, but no proof, yet."

"Too bad you'll die before the case gets solved."

He aimed the knife from his shoulder.

She swept her left hand from under the blanket, as the blade plunged toward her heart.

She rammed the fingernail file into his right eye. His screams assaulted her ears. Her right foot kicked into his groin sending him sailing to the floor.

He cried and moaned as he tugged the file.

Lexie high-stepped over Brody's body. She swung the door open as Tye banged.

"Lexie?" Tye puffed.

"Call security, Brody attacked me."

Within five minutes, six men ran down the hall toward her. "Get him to the infirmary before he bleeds to death," she directed.

Two men lifted Brody's feet. Another guard held under his armpits, with Brody's head supported against the guy's chest.

Sampson calmed the cruisers who stood in doorways.

Tye closed the door. "How did you take him, Sis?"

"A girl uses whatever weapon that's available. Thank goodness I filed my nails before Delia's wedding. I used my trusty fingernail file."

"Be prepared is certainly your motto."

"You know it, Bro."

Tye rubbed his temples. "I'm glad we can put these murders behind us."

"Mabel's case isn't solved."

"I thought Brody killed her."

"I think there are one or two murders he didn't commit."

"Schwinn had access to her room. He claimed the maid found Mabel, but the maid turned down the covers before she arrived from the show. Likely he set up Sampson—only reason to assign his bigoted mother an Afro-American attendant. Trace evidence in the room won't result in an arrest since he's her son."

"Not sounding conclusive."

"Maybe he left a fingerprint on my room key or on the knife Brody was supposed to kill me with."

"Which proves an assisted breakout, not murder."

"I know, Tye, but he won't confess. One thing for sure, the life insurance company will ride his ass to prove he doesn't qualify for the inheritance. I have confidence his day will come. I'm glad the problem belongs to the FBI and not me. How about we try to get a little sleep?"

"I'm for that."

CHAPTER THIRTY-SEVEN

Lexie marveled at the clouds outside the airplane window. They were like giant cotton balls. She felt the urge to reach out and touch the softness.

Soon her thoughts strayed back to the cruise. The FBI took custody of Brody and escorted him to federal prison. The rest of the wedding trip was uneventful.

She caught a glimpse of officers surrounding Schwinn when she exited the ship in Fort Lauderdale. She didn't know the charge, but was glad they were at least suspicious of his actions.

Soon after she stepped off the ship, an email arrived from Judge Marcus Simpson. He ordered the siblings to report the minute they reached Diffee.

The urgency of the red lettered message tightened her chest. It was more than her probable firing. Her worse fear was that Tye would get arrested for Wilbur Langley's murder.

···•••●●●••···

Sloan arranged the bags in the trunk, then drove to Diffee. Upon arrival the siblings threw their bags in the back of Tye's truck,

"Where are you headed?" Sloan questioned.

"Judge Simpson summoned us to the courthouse. Jamie will meet us there with Sky."

Delia waved, "Good luck."

"We need it," Tye harrumphed.

"Glad we're on dry land." Lexie said.

Her brother's speed sent poofs of dust around the vehicle. "Do you think the judge is still at the courthouse?"

Tye slowed for a turn. "I hope so. The suspense is killing me."

Worry bubbled in Lexie's stomach. "We may wish we stayed on the ship."

"Too late now. There's the courthouse."

Pole lights lit the way as they jogged across the front lawn.

Lexie rapped on Judge Simpson's office door.

"Come in."

"Do you still want visitors? It's late."

"I purposely waited."

"Thanks—I guess."

"Based on testimony from witnesses, and the recapture of Brody, the court has ruled that Lexie and Tye Wolfe are innocent of wrong doing in Brody Wolfe's escape. Furthermore, you two are directed to return to your positions as sheriff and deputy sheriff, as soon as possible."

"Thank you, Judge. This means so much."

"Thought you'd also like to know that Houser found Wilbur's killer—Slick Sims."

The tightness in her chest released. "How did he figure it out?"

"Didn't take any detective work. Slick thought Clayton was like him—a crook. He admitted that he killed Wilbur. He figured Tye would get charged with the murder and you discredited. Clayton's an honest man—he told Houser."

She started to shake Simpson's hand, but gave him a hug instead. "Thank you."

"Don't thank me yet. Slick was sheriff for a few days. There's probably messes you'll have to cleanup. Let's get out of here, long day."

Tye's words shot out, "When do I get Gabriel?"

"Too late for all that paperwork tonight. We'll deal with that problem later in the week."

Tye hesitated, "But...."

"No buts, it's late and I'm tired."

Out of Simpson's earshot, Lexie acknowledged Tye's crestfallen face. "I'm sure he'll process Gabriel's case soon."

Tye grumbled, "Didn't sound like it."

A blast of "welcome home" hit their ears as they walked across the courthouse lawn.

Lexie squeezed Sky and smooched each cheek.

Seth, Adam and Jamie trapped Tye in a family hug.

Gabriel's head popped up from his hiding place. "DADDY, I'M HOME!"

The two ran toward each other. Tye swung him in the air then kissed his forehead.

"About time you came home, son. Were you captured by space creatures?"

"Oh, Daddy! You're silly."

BOOKS BY
Donna Welch Jones

Sheriff Lexie Wolfe Novels

Killing the Secret

Deadly Search

Terror's Grip

Murder & Beyond

Deranged Justice

Her Dying Message

NEW RELEASE
UNBREAK THEIR HEARTS
Women's Suspense